CHAPTER ONE

"The definition of evil, is something which is profoundly immoral and wicked."

The Year 11 class of Vazon High weren't paying much attention to the droning voice of Mr Graham. The aging English teacher wasn't a gifted public speaker, and the monotonous tone of his voice was somewhat sleep-inducing. In fact, more than one of the students in the class had dozed off in the morning heat of the classroom.

"In its noun form *evil* is defined as someone who is morally reprehensible." Mr Graham hadn't quite finished yet. "Or it can be an act that is sinful arising from what can be considered bad character. James Green, are you even listening?"

The sixteen-year-old wasn't. His eyes were closed and his mouth was wide open. He was snoring rather loudly.

"James," Mr Graham shouted. "Wake up."

A few of the students started to laugh. James Green opened one eye.

"Eh?"

"Give me an example of evil," Mr Graham said.

"Evil?" James repeated.

"Falling asleep in class may not be considered evil, but it is still something I will not tolerate. Well? Do you have an example of evil you'd like to share with the rest of the class?"

"No."

James said this with such finality it left the experienced English teacher speechless for a moment.

"Anyone else?" Mr Graham asked after a few seconds. "Can anyone else offer up an example of evil?"

"Adolf Hitler," a girl in the front row put forward.

"Very good. And why do you believe Adolf Hitler to be evil?"

"He was a megalomaniac and a sociopath. He brainwashed an entire nation to fulfil his own delusional ideals. He wasn't doing it for the good of the country – he was working to a purely personal agenda. That's what makes him evil."

"Do what?" a boy in the back row said. "I need Google Translate to figure out what you just said."

"That's enough, Michael," Mr Graham said. "What Sasha is suggesting is that Adolf Hitler wasn't concerned about the future of Germany when he did what he did. Sasha is implying that he killed millions of people to satisfy his own depraved desires."

"It wasn't implied, Mr Graham," the girl called Sasha argued. "I was stating a fact."

"Who else can give me an example of evil?" Mr Graham said. "James? Have you woken up sufficiently to partake in the class? Give me one example – that's not too much to ask, is it?"

James looked straight at him. His eyes were unblinking, and his stare was relentless. Mr Graham looked away.

"My mother," James said.

"What?" Mr Graham asked.

"You wanted me to give you an example of evil," James elaborated. "I'm giving you one. My mother is pure evil."

"I think we've exhausted this topic of conversation. Let's move on."

James ignored him. "She's evil because she killed my dad. She murdered my father and left him where she knew I would find him."

CHAPTER TWO

Detective Inspector Liam O'Reilly was in a great mood. Things were going well for him for the first time in weeks. His leg was slowly recovering after the motorbike accident that left him with a broken femur. He still relied on the stick much of the time but the bone was definitely getting stronger and at the last check-up the doctor had informed him it would soon recover completely and he would be able to do everything he'd done prior to the accident.

He had a woman in his life he could quite easily imagine spending the rest of his days with. Victoria Radcliffe had burst into O'Reilly's life and stayed put. The laryngeal cancer she was suffering wasn't yet under control, but the medical professionals were confident she would make a full recovery in time. She'd undergone a course of radiation therapy and it had proven to be successful. O'Reilly and Victoria had made up their minds that they were going to beat this thing, and they believed they would. In an unorthodox turn of events, Victora had proposed to the Irishman, and O'Reilly had answered in the affirmative.

Even the cats weren't as annoying as they usually were. Bram and Juliet were being uncharacteristically nice to O'Reilly and this made him suspicious. The portly ginger tom and the slender black lady had been on their best behaviour for weeks, but O'Reilly knew he couldn't afford to let his guard down. He knew there was always an ulterior motive where cats were concerned.

It was a glorious Thursday morning on the island of Guernsey. The balmy late-June weather promised another warm summer, and this was reflected in the mood of the people who called the island home. O'Reilly had a day off and the high spirits he was feeling had even inspired him to look online for a possible replacement for the Honda Rebel that had been written off in the accident. He was still in two minds about getting back on a motorbike but, as Victoria had pointed out, the odds of being involved in another accident were definitely in his favour now. O'Reilly wasn't so sure.

Bram and Juliet strolled in. The cats were inseparable. Bram inspected his food bowl, determined there was still nothing in it but cat food, and paid it no more attention.

"Cat food," O'Reilly told him. "It's what cats eat. Get used to it."

He had a day off today and he wasn't sure how he was going to spend it. Victoria was working at the bike shop she co-owned with her brother Tommy, and he didn't want to disturb her there. He contemplated giving his daughter a ring but decided not to. Assumpta was at work too. She'd been with the Guernsey Gazette for over a year now and O'Reilly didn't want to bother her either.

He settled for a short walk. The sun was out and there weren't many clouds in the sky. He'd been walking more and more since the doctors had told him it would speed up his recovery. He picked up his phone and his gaze fell on the stick against the wall in the hallway of the apartment.

"Stick or no stick?" he debated.

He picked it up and headed for the door. He'd got used to the stick and it wouldn't hurt to take it with him.

"Baby steps," he told nobody in particular.

He followed La Grange east and soon reached the entrance to the harbour. He stopped to watch the ferries coming in from England and France. Soon the population of the island would double and, if the weather forecasters had got it right they could expect a long, dry summer. Guernsey came alive in the summer and O'Reilly felt it too. The restaurants and hotels would do a roaring trade in the upcoming months.

He turned left onto the esplanade and followed the road until he reached the first turnoff to the beach. He stepped onto the sand and contemplated taking off his shoes and socks. He opted not to. His feet hadn't seen the sun for a very long time and they weren't suitable to be revealed in public. The long thin beach was packed with people, and O'Reilly didn't have the heart to subject them to the sight of his Irish feet.

He stopped for a breather on one of the benches down from the esplanade and his phone started to ring as soon as he'd taken the weight off his feet. The screen told him it was work and for the first time since he could remember he decided to ignore it. The sun on his face felt good and whatever the phone call was about could wait. He wasn't the only detective employed by the Island Police, and he was enjoying the time on the beach.

The phone stopped ringing and immediately started again. O'Reilly found his settings and turned it on silent. He looked out to sea, and something flew past his head. Shortly afterwards a girl who looked to be about ten approached him.

"Sorry about that," she said.

She walked past him and went to retrieve the frisbee.

"Do you want to play?" she said when she came back.

"I'm afraid my frisbee playing days are over," O'Reilly said.

"You're not that old."

"I'll take that as a compliment. But there must be someone better you can find to chuck that thing around with you."

"There isn't. My brother thinks it's for kids. He's thirteen."

"What's your name?" O'Reilly asked her.

"Lauren."

"That's a very pretty name. Where are your parents?"

"Being boring. They're sleeping over there."

She pointed in the direction of the shore.

"Why aren't you at school?" O'Reilly said.

"It's the holidays," Lauren said. "I don't go back until September."

O'Reilly wasn't aware that the schools had broken up yet. He mentioned this to Lauren.

"I go to school in France," she explained. "It's a private school and they break up before the other schools. And now I'm stuck on this island with nobody to play with. Some holiday. There's my brother now." She said goodbye and ran off with her frisbee.

O'Reilly smiled. It was the first time he'd been asked to throw a frisbee around by a young child and it gave him a warm feeling in his stomach. Lauren had reached her brother now and it appeared he'd changed his mind about how childish the frisbee was. O'Reilly watched as it was thrown in his direction, deftly caught and thrown back.

He got up off the bench and something fell out of his pocket as he did so. His mobile phone landed on the sand by his feet. O'Reilly picked it up and dusted it off. He was about to put it in his pocket when he thought about the earlier missed calls. He swiped the screen and turned it back on. The ringtone sounded two seconds later.

"O'Reilly," he answered it.

"Sorry to bother you, sir." It was DC Owen.

"What is it, Katie?"

"We got a call from Vazon High School. One of the teachers called us after a student said something in class. The year 11 boy told the whole class that his father had been murdered and it was his mother who killed him."

"Sounds like a schoolboy prank to me," O'Reilly said. "The teacher didn't seem to think so. The boy was acting really strange. He refused to leave the school because of what was waiting for him at home. The school tried to contact the parents but neither of them answered their phones. The English teacher was convinced there was something to it, so we sent some uniforms round to the boy's house to put his mind at ease."

"And?"

"He was telling the truth, sir," DC Owen said. "The front door was locked, but they spotted someone in the hallway. He wasn't moving. They broke the lock on the door and went in. It's a bloodbath in there. Early accounts suggest the boy's father was stabbed at least a dozen times."

CHAPTER THREE

O'Reilly got out of DC Owen's car and looked at the house they were parked outside. He still wasn't allowed to drive and DC Owen had picked him up from the esplanade. Two police cars and an ambulance were parked further up the road. DI Peters' car was also there. The house on Rue La Mere looked extremely expensive. The double-storey property was situated one road from the main beach road and O'Reilly reckoned they would have a spectacular view over Vazon Bay from the second floor. The front garden was very large and it was clear someone had taken good care of it. The lawn looked like a golf course, and the shrubs and trees had been well maintained. The family who lived here were obviously not short of cash.

"How the other half live," DC Owen said. "You don't want to know how much these places cost."
"You're right, Katie," O'Reilly said. "I don't want to know, and I don't care. What else do we know?"
"The Vazon High schoolboy is called James Green. Apparently the English class were discussing the concept of evil and the teacher asked them for examples of it. James Green told the whole class that his mother was evil because she killed his dad and left him where she knew James would find him."
"Good Lord," O'Reilly said. "What makes the boy think his mother killed his father?"
"We don't know yet."
"Where is the mother now?"
"We've been unable to locate her," DC Owen said. "She doesn't work, and none of her friends seem to know where she is."

"Keep looking. Why on earth would a schoolboy think his mother killed his father?"

DI Peters emerged from the house and walked towards the front gate. The Head of Forensics made a beeline for his car. O'Reilly walked over to him.

"Morning, Jim," he said. "What have we got in there?"

"Dead male," DI Peters said. "He was lying face down in the hallway. I'd estimate he died due to blood loss. There was a lot of blood on the carpet. It looks like he's been repeatedly stabbed in the chest, neck and face. There was a hell of a lot of fury in this attack."

"Did you find the murder weapon?"

"Not a sausage. There's a knife block in the kitchen. One of the knives is missing. If I'm not mistaken it was the paring knife. Very sharp. The perpetrator must have taken it with him."

"Her," O'Reilly corrected. "The schoolboy seems to think his mother did this."

"That's what I heard too. Whoever killed him wanted him dead, that's for sure. There's little doubt about that. I need to get back inside. We've got a lot of work still to do. I only came out to fetch some things from the car."

"I'll leave you to it," O'Reilly said.

"Do you think the boy was telling the truth?" DC Owen asked.

"There's no way of knowing until we speak to him," O'Reilly said. "And the woman needs to be found. I want everyone focusing on that. It's very suspicious that she's disappeared into thin air just after her husband is murdered."

"It is," DC Owen agreed. "Sorry about your day off."

"It is what it is. Do we know anything else about the family? Does the boy have any siblings?"

"He has an older sister," DC Owen informed him. "According to the English teacher she's in the sixth form. Or she was. She's just completed her A Levels and she's on holiday somewhere in southeast Asia now."

"I don't like this, Katie. What could possibly make a sixteen-year-old boy think his mother has killed his father?"

"And why blurt it out to the whole class?" DC Owen added.

"Where is he now?"

"Still at school. He refused to leave."

"That's our first port of call then," O'Reilly decided. "I want to know what he has to tell us. And I want his mother found."

DI Peters came back outside. He walked straight over to O'Reilly.

"I want your opinion on something."

"Shoot," O'Reilly said.

"You have to come and see this for yourself."

O'Reilly managed to squeeze himself into a SOC suit that was two sizes too small and followed the Head of Forensics inside number 2 Rue La Mere. DS Henry Earle was taking photographs of the position of the body in the hallway. He nodded a greeting to O'Reilly and carried on snapping away.

The interior of the house was just as O'Reilly expected it to be judging by the grandeur outside. The wooden hallway was dotted with expensive looking carpets. The dead man was laid on one of them and O'Reilly knew they would never be able to clean the blood off it. There was a lot of it, and it had soaked right into the thick pile.

DI Peters carried on walking and stopped outside a room to the left. The door was wide open and when O'Reilly looked inside he saw it was a large sitting room. The bookcases stood all the way to the ceiling and all the shelves were full of books. A huge window took up almost all of one of the walls. It looked out onto a section of the garden. A swimming pool was sparkling in the late morning sun.

"What is it you wanted to show me?" O'Reilly asked.

"A few things," DI Peters replied. "The first of them is in here. What do you make of that?"

He took out a pen and tapped on the wood of one of the bookcases. O'Reilly stepped closer to get a better look.

"It looks like blood."

"I think it is," DI Peters agreed. "And it looks fresh."

"Are those prints?"

"They are. We've got some pics, and we've taken some imprints. That's when I realised what's wrong with this part of the bookcase."

"It looks like any old bookcase to me," O'Reilly said.

"That's because it's supposed to. Pick a book."

O'Reilly frowned. "What?"

"Pick a book," DI Peters said. "Any book."

O'Reilly humoured him. He selected an anthology of Victorian literature and tried to remove it. He couldn't.

"What the devil."

"It's a false bookcase," DI Peters explained. "This part is anyway. The rest of it appears to be the real deal. I think there's a hidden room behind it."

"Have you managed to have a look?"

"I can't figure out how to open it. But I'm positive this is a false door that leads to a hidden room. If you tap on the wood of the spines of the books, it's hollow. I thought it was strange that all the books are exactly the same size. There is something behind it."

"Do you think the mother might be hiding in there?"

"I called out," DI Peters said. "But nobody replied. And I put my ear to the fake books and couldn't hear a thing."

"Let me know when you manage to get it open."

"You'll be the first to know."

"What else did you want to show me?" O'Reilly asked.

"It's something upstairs," DI Peters said. "In the master bedroom."

He left the sitting room and led O'Reilly up two flights of stairs. The master bedroom took up almost the entire floor. It was big enough to play a game of squash inside while someone else was playing snooker in the other half of the room. It was the biggest bedroom O'Reilly had ever laid eyes on.

He told DI Peters as much.

"It is a bit excessive, isn't it?" he said. "Especially when you consider the fact that only one person sleeps in here. I'll show you."

He walked towards the bed. On one of the bedside tables was a selection of paperbacks. They were all romantic adventure books. Next to them was a tub of something.

"Night cream," DI Peters said. "Probably cost more than we earn in a week. There's nothing on the other bedside table and nothing in the cupboard. Only one person sleeps in this bed."

"This is obviously the wife's side of the bed," O'Reilly deduced. "But perhaps her husband didn't read in bed, and just because there's nothing on the table doesn't mean he doesn't sleep here."

DI Peters shook his head. "I checked the ensuite bathroom. There's only one toothbrush, and the shampoos and other toiletries are all ones a woman would use."

O'Reilly thought about this for a moment.

"Did you check the other bedrooms? It's possible they slept in separate beds."

"The other bedrooms are on the ground floor," DI Peters told him. "Four of them. Two are clearly the rooms of teenagers."

"They have a girl and a boy," O'Reilly said. "That makes sense."

"And the other two haven't been slept in for a very long time. There is nothing in either of them to suggest the husband has been staying in one of them. I don't think he was living here."

"What was he doing here then?" O'Reilly wondered. "If he doesn't live here, what was he doing here and why did he end up dead here?"

CHAPTER FOUR

O'Reilly didn't even know Vazon High School existed. It was one of a number of prestigious private schools on the island, and judging by the cars in the car park outside it was clear that only the offspring of the well-heeled attended. It never ceased to amaze O'Reilly how much money was concentrated in such a small chunk of land.

"What school did you go to, Katie?" he asked DC Owen.

"It was nothing like this place, sir," she said. "Just an ordinary comprehensive in Carmel. My dad would never have been able to afford something like this on a police salary."

"Where do all the students come from? I wouldn't have thought there were enough kids on the island."

"A lot of foreigners send their children to school in Guernsey. French, German, Dutch. They think by giving them an education here will give them an early advantage in life. Not that they need it. The kids who go to schools like these probably never actually have to work. There's far too much money in far too few hands."

"It's the way of the world," O'Reilly said. "Is someone expecting us?"

"I called ahead and Mr Graham, the English teacher has agreed to speak to us."

"I want to talk to the boy."

"The teacher seems to think we can't talk to him without an adult present," DC Owen told him.

"Then he has a lot to learn about the law, Katie. A serious crime has been committed. The boy is a prime witness, and we're well within our rights to haul him in and formally interview him."

"Can I make a suggestion, sir?"

"Of course."

"I don't think dragging him to the station is a good idea right now," DC Owen said. "Maybe later, but he'll be more likely to tell us what he knows without the stress of the formality of the station."

"I don't want the teacher involved. He has nothing to do with this."

"Then we'll explain that to him. We'll ask if we can talk to the boy somewhere private."

"You're probably right," O'Reilly said. "As always. Let's go and get some answers."

After waiting to be buzzed in through the main entrance to the school O'Reilly and DC Owen were escorted to the English department. Mr Graham was waiting for them inside his office. James Green was nowhere to be seen.

Mr Graham stood up when they came in and offered his hand to O'Reilly. The Irish detective ignored it.

"We're here to speak to James Green," he said instead.

"I've prepared a classroom for you," Mr Graham said. "James is waiting in there."

"Grand. Could you show us where it is?"

"Of course. And I'll be sitting in during the questioning."

"No," O'Reilly said. "No, you won't."

"You cannot possibly interrogate a sixteen-year-old boy without an adult present. His father is dead and his mother is missing – he has no other family on the island, so I will step in on their behalf."

"We need to speak to him alone," DC Owen informed him.

"You're not allowed to do that."

"I assure you, we are," O'Reilly said. "We appreciate your concern, but this is a police matter now, and the school is no longer involved."

"This is outrageous. I want to speak to your boss."

O'Reilly sighed and nodded.

He turned to DC Owen. "Katie, do you have the number for Superintendent Hayes?"

"Of course, sir," she said.

She opened her phone. "Do you have a piece of paper?"

Mr Graham handed her a notepad, and DC Owen wrote the number on it.

"Superintendent Hayes may not answer straight away," O'Reilly told the English teacher. "She's currently on maternity leave. She's expecting a baby very soon, but if you leave a message I'm sure she'll get back to you."

"OK," Mr Graham said. "Just don't upset him. James has been through enough and here at Vazon High we take the welfare of our students very seriously."

"I'll bear that in mind," O'Reilly said. "But this is a murder investigation, and sometimes we have to ask difficult questions to get to the truth. We've already wasted enough time. Could you please point us in the direction of the boy?"

James Green was alone in the classroom when they went inside. He was sitting at one of the desks, staring out of the window. A game of football was in progress on the field outside. O'Reilly pulled up a chair and sat opposite the teenager. DC Owen said next to him.

"James," O'Reilly began. "I'm DI O'Reilly and this is DC Owen. You know why we're here, don't you?"
James didn't even look at him. He continued to gaze out of the window.
"Who's winning?" O'Reilly asked him.
James shrugged his shoulders.

"James," O'Reilly said. "Tell us what you told the English class earlier."
"Why?"
O'Reilly wasn't expecting this.
"You were discussing the concept of evil," DC Owen said. "Is that right?"
James nodded his head.
"What did the discussion involve?" O'Reilly said.

"I can't remember."

"Mr Graham, your English teacher phoned the police, James," O'Reilly said. "He phoned the police because he was concerned about something you said in class. You said your mother was evil because she killed your dad. When we went to check it out, what you told the class was confirmed - someone had killed your father. We've yet to determine who did that, but we need you to answer our questions."

"I don't know anything," James said.

"OK," O'Reilly said. "Let's go back a bit. What made you say that in class? What made you tell the class that your mother killed your father?"

"Because it had to be her."

"Why do you think that?" DC Owen said.

"Who else could have done it?"

"When was the last time you saw your father?" O'Reilly said.

James looked him in the eyes. "This morning. I got up and found him dead in the hallway."

"Why didn't you call someone?" DC Owen said. "Why didn't you call the police?"

"I don't know. I was late for school I suppose."

"And you just left him there?" O'Reilly said.

"He was dead," James told him. "What else could I do for him?"

O'Reilly remembered something DC Owen had told him in the phone call earlier.

"When our officers went to your house, the door was locked. Was it you who locked the door?"

"Probably," James said.

"You found your father murdered. He'd sustained multiple stab wounds and he was covered in blood. Are you telling me you left him there and went straight to school? After locking the front door?"

"I must have."

"When we were at the house earlier," O'Reilly said. "We found something in the sitting room. The room where all the bookcases are."

"I know where the sitting room is," James said.

"One of our forensics officers stumbled upon what looked like a fake part of the bookcase. He believes there is a hidden room behind it. Do you know anything about that?"

"It's news to me."

"Are you saying that when we do manage to gain access to whatever is behind that bookcase you'll still tell us you didn't know it was there?"

"I have no idea what you're talking about."

O'Reilly wasn't sure what else to ask. He couldn't figure out the boy's behaviour. He was either suffering from the effects of shock or something else was going on.

"Why do you think it was your mother who did this, James?" he asked.

"It's the only logical explanation."

"Did they not get on?" DC Owen said.

"They've been separated for two months."

"Does your father not live with you?" O'Reilly said.

"He has an apartment in St Peter Port."

This tied in with what DI Peters suspected about only one person sleeping in the main bedroom.

"What was he doing at your house?" O'Reilly said.

"I don't know," James said.

"When was the last time you saw your dad before this morning?" DC Owen asked.

"Last weekend."

"And you don't know why he came to the house?" O'Reilly said.

"There's only one logical explanation," James said.

"And what would that be?" O'Reilly pressed.

James stared out of the window again. "My mother arranged to meet him there so she could kill him."

CHAPTER FIVE

"We've had no joy with the mother," DS Skinner informed O'Reilly.

He'd come back to the station after the bizarre conversation at Vazon High. James Green was still at school. The Head of School had agreed to let him board there for the foreseeable future. The student accommodation wasn't full and there were a few rooms free. They'd tried to get hold of James's older sister but so far they hadn't been able to locate her.

"We've spoken to some of Mrs Green's friends," DS Skinner continued. "And none of them have seen her for a few days."

"What about her phone?" O'Reilly said.

"Voicemail every time. She's either switched it off, or she's ignoring calls."

"Have you checked points of entry and exit?"

"It's the next thing on the list, sir. It's going to take time to go through all the channels."

"Prioritise," O'Reilly said. "Her phone is important. Find out who her service provider is and look at her incoming and outgoing calls. I want to know if she called her estranged husband recently. The airport and the ferry terminals can wait."

"What did the boy tell you?" DS Skinner asked.

"I didn't know what to make of him," O'Reilly said. "He's either in shock or something else is going on. Something nasty. He's convinced that his mother killed his father, but he couldn't explain why he thinks that."

"Are we going to bring him in for a formal interview?"

"We will," O'Reilly confirmed. "But I want to know more before we go that route. What are the others up to?"

"Andy is still busy with the list of friends we managed to find out about. Theresa Green has a lot of them, and every time we speak to one of them, more names get added to the list. Katie is concentrating on her car. The vehicle wasn't parked in the garage where it usually is, so it's safe to assume she's driving it. We've put the word out, but so far we haven't had a single sighting. We're doing everything we can to find her."

"This is a small island, Will," O'Reilly reminded him. "It is not easy to hide here. I want that woman found."

He left DS Skinner to it and headed for his office. He needed a cup of tea in his belly. He'd just switched on the kettle when his phone started to ring. It was Superintendent Hayes.

"Ma'am," O'Reilly answered it. "How's maternity leave treating you?"

"I'll be glad when I pop this thing out to be honest."

"Is there something you need me for?" O'Reilly asked.

"I've just got off the phone with a rather irate English teacher."

"Mr Graham. I didn't think he'd actually phone you."

"What's going on, Liam?"

O'Reilly told her. He told her about the dead man and the son's suspicions about his mother.

"Why would James think his mother was responsible?" Superintendent Hayes said when O'Reilly had finished bringing her up to date.

"I don't know," O'Reilly said. "I really don't know what to make of the boy. He claims he found his father dead and then he went to school. We only got wind of it because the kid blurted it out in class. It's a strange one."

"What do we have from a forensics perspective?"

"It's early days," O'Reilly replied. "Jim is still at the house. The body has been taken away so we'll have an idea of the timescale involved when Dr Lille has examined him, but right now I'm putting all our efforts into finding the mother. She's disappeared and I want to know why she's disappeared."

"Is it possible she's suffered the same fate as her husband?"

"I did consider that," O'Reilly said. "It's possible whoever killed Mr Green also killed his estranged wife, but why leave only one of them behind? If you're going to try and get away with murder, you dispose of the bodies. You do not leave one of them on display for a teenager to find."

"What else did the boy tell you?"

"Not enough."

"Did you ask him if he heard anything during the night?"

"That can wait until the formal interview," O'Reilly said. "But I want to be armed with more info before we do that."

"Is the boy a suspect?"

"He most certainly is," O'Reilly confirmed. "He had opportunity, but we need to get some more ducks in a row before we put that to him. I won't keep you any longer. You must have a lot to do."

"I don't. I'm going spare at home. Tom is driving me crazy. When he's not at work he's treating me like I might break at any moment. Is there any chance you can request his help with the investigation?"

"I'll see what I can do. How long is it now?"

"I'm due in a couple of weeks," Superintendent Hayes told him.

"I'll keep you up to date," O'Reilly said.

They said their goodbyes and ended the call.

O'Reilly made the tea and sat down at his desk. He tried to make sense of what had happened in Vazon. A teenage boy had told the entire class that his father had been murdered by his mother. The man had sustained over a dozen stab wounds to the chest, face and neck and he'd been left in the hallway of a house he no longer lived in. O'Reily knew he wouldn't be able to decide on a course of action until he knew more about the victim. He brought his laptop to life and waited for it to warm up.

When it did he keyed the victim's name into the task bar and an entire page of results appeared on the screen. Arnold Green's family came from old money – that much was clear from the first couple of sites his name came up on. His wealth was generational. His grandfather had started a tour operation company in the late forties. His son had taken over the business in the early eighties and he'd sold it at the height of its success. At the time of the sale the company owned sixteen passenger ferries and a fleet of aircraft. The business was sold for almost forty-million pounds.

According to another article on the web, Arnold Green was an only child and he inherited the lot.

James Green's father was an incredibly wealthy man, and O'Reilly knew this was the starting point in the investigation. Who stood to gain from Arnold Green's demise? O'Reilly sensed that there was more to it than that, but it was early days, and right now he knew they needed to follow the money.

CHAPTER SIX

John Hillman looked out of the window onto the garden and sighed. The grass needed mowing. The gardener had promised he would cut it and it was obvious he hadn't. The flower beds were also untidy, and John decided enough was enough. Gardeners were difficult to find on the island and that's why he'd tolerated the old boy who tended to the acre of land at the back of the property, but he'd had enough. The gardener's contract would be terminated the next time he came to the house.

The pool was also looking rather shabby, and John knew he would have to have a word with the pool boy about that. There was nothing worse than a green swimming pool. All of that could wait though. John had a rare day off and he was planning on spending the afternoon on the golf course a few miles away. Eighteen holes and a few drinks at the clubhouse afterwards. Perhaps he would get a bite to eat there as well.

He'd recently treated himself to a brand-new set of golf clubs. A full set of Calloway Pro clubs that had set him back more than thirty thousand pounds. It was money well spent and John was looking forward to seeing what they played like. The salesman at the shop in Scotland had assured him that if these clubs didn't improve his game he would be refunded half the cost. John was keen to take him at his word.

A noise downstairs caused him to turn his attention away from the garden. It sounded like someone had opened the front door. John listened carefully but heard nothing more. He must have imagined it. Then he heard it again – a quiet tapping sound. He left the bedroom and emerged onto the landing.

"Is anyone there?"

Nothing.

He started to walk downstairs. The tapping sound could be heard once more.

"Who's down there?"

Nobody replied.

"Amanda," he cried out. "Is that you?"

He couldn't remember what day the cleaning lady came to the house, but he was sure she wasn't due at work today.

He reached the bottom step and looked around. There didn't appear to be anybody there.

"This isn't funny," he said.

He'd heard about the murder of Arnold Green via a knock on the door earlier that morning. Two uniformed officers had asked him if he'd heard anything during the night. John had told them that he'd slept soundly and they'd left it at that. He wondered if they were back to ask more questions. But if that was the case surely, they'd knock on the door again. They wouldn't just walk inside the house.

He looked at the golf bag propped up against the wall by the front door. There was something odd about it. He recalled placing it there earlier, ready for when he set off for the golf course, but he was sure he'd placed it to the left of the door. Now it stood on the right-hand side, below the window.

There was something else not quite right about it. The zip on the side was open. He knew for a fact he'd zipped it up, ready to be picked up and taken to the car. Someone had opened it.

"Who's there?" he asked. "Whoever it is, come out now or you'll be sorry."

Somebody coughed and then John heard another noise. It was the sound of footsteps on the parquet floor – rapid steps getting closer. John turned around just in time to see the head of the Calloway number 9 iron flying towards his face. There was a crack as the bones in his nose shattered and John screamed. The expensive golf club came down again, this time on the top of John's head. Flashes of light exploded, and he felt a white-hot pain shoot down the side of his face. He fell backwards onto the floor and banged his head hard on the shiny surface of the hallway. He experienced a brief feeling of confusion when he realised who was holding his brand-new golf club before the final blow obliterated all sensation.

* * *

"Please tell me one of you has something to report."
O'Reilly looked at the faces inside the briefing room. Two men and one woman – that was the extent of the team right now. Three extremely competent police detectives O'Reilly had grown to like. Even DC Andy Stone had his rare moments of insight. The rat-faced DC had surprised O'Reilly on the odd occasion.

He was about to do so once more.
"I found the car, sir."
"Which car are we talking about, Andy?" O'Reilly asked him.

"Theresa Green's Audi. I made a list of the places she liked to frequent. Restaurants, clubs and the like and I tracked the car down to the tennis club in Les Martins."

"How on earth did you know where she liked to hang out?"

"It was the first question I asked her friends," DC Stone explained. "Apparently she played tennis in Les Martins three times a week. I drove out there and the Audi was parked in the car park."

"Good thinking."

"That's all I found, sir," DC Stone said. "Mrs Green wasn't at the club, and none of the staff or the members who were there have seen her since last Sunday."

"Why would she park the car there?" DC Owen wondered. "Why park the car and leave it there if she's not playing tennis?"

"The tennis club has CCTV covering the car park," DC Stone carried on. "But the security guard has the day off today, and I couldn't find anyone else who had access to the camera footage."

"Has the security guard been informed of how important that footage is?" O'Reilly asked.

"He was out shopping with his wife," DC Stone said. "But he's promised to make a special trip to Les Martins to get us the footage. Three hours, he said."

"You're in fine form today, Andy," O'Reilly said. "Good work."

DC Stone grinned, revealing his recent dental work.

"Anything else?" O'Reilly asked.

The ensuing silence told him there wasn't anything else to report.

"Right," he said. "I did some digging of my own and I found out that our dead man was worth a good few bob. Arnold Green's father sold his business for forty-million pounds and Arnold inherited the lot."

"Perhaps someone had forty million reasons for wanting him dead," DS Stone said.

"I wouldn't quite put it like that, Andy," O'Reilly said. "But yes, we have a very strong motive here. It's very possible he was killed for that money. I want to know who stands to gain now he's no longer breathing. Check out insurance policies and see if we can gain access to his Last Will and Testament. We know he wasn't yet divorced. He was separated from his wife, but according to the law they were still married. Are there any other mystery beneficiaries we don't know about?"

"Are you suggesting this was about money?" DS Skinner asked.

"It's an age-old motive for murder, Will. I'm just looking at all the obvious ones first. Who stands to benefit from Arnold Green's death? That's what we need to find out."

"What about the wife?" DC Stone said. "Aren't we going to keep looking for her?"

"Yes and no."

"Sir?"

"It seems to me that Mrs Green has gone to a lot of effort to stay hidden," O'Reilly said. "And if that's the case it's going to be difficult to find her. We'll come back to that after we've looked into Mr Green's finances."

"Do we have any idea of the timeline involved?" DS Skinner asked.

"Not yet," O'Reilly said. "We'll know more after the postmortem. Forensics ought to have more information for us during the course of the day too. I didn't get a detailed look at the scene, but from what I did see it didn't look like the killer stuck around. There was no blood anywhere inside the house apart from in the hallway. It's likely the killer carried out the murder and left the house straight afterwards. I want someone from forensics to get over to Les Martins to see if they can get into Mrs Green's car, and I want to know who stands to benefit from Arnold Green's death before the afternoon briefing. On you go."

CHAPTER SEVEN

"James. Is there anything I can get you?"
James Green wasn't listening. The Vazon High student was sitting on the bed in his room. Violent guitar music could be heard through the headphones he was wearing.

"James," Kelly Powell stepped into the room. "Can I get you anything?"

James looked up at her but he didn't remove the headphones.

Kelly tapped her ears as an indication he should take them off. James slipped one of them away from his ear.

"What?"

"Do you need anything?" Kelly asked. "Are you feeling OK?"

Kelly Powell was the French teacher at the school. An ex-Vazon High student, Kelly had taken a job at the school immediately after qualifying as a teacher.

"I want my mother," James told her.

"The police are looking for her," Kelly said.

"I want my mother," James said again. "I want to know why she killed my dad."

"I think we should get you to the hospital."

"Don't bother."

"You should have been checked over by a doctor," Kelly said. "You've had a terrible shock."

"Just go away."

"I'm only trying to help."

"You can help me by bringing my mother here," James said. "If you can't do that, you can go away."

With that he replaced the headphone over his left ear. The music was turned up, and the French teacher knew she was wasting her time.

She left him alone with his music and went outside. It was early afternoon and the late-June sun was beating down on the sports field. A couple of girls were running round the athletics track. More students were busy with a game of softball further across the field. Kelly walked back towards the main school building.

She was halfway there when someone called out behind her.

"Miss Powell."

Kelly turned around and saw it was Sasha Hillman. She walked over and took off her sunglasses.

"How is he? How's James?"

"I think he's still in shock," Kelly said.

"He really freaked us out in class," Sasha said. "All that business about his mum killing his dad, but it's true, isn't it?"

"We don't know what happened yet. Nobody knows."

"But James's dad is dead, isn't he?" Sasha said. "That part is true."

"It is," Kelly admitted.

"Can I go and talk to him?"

"I don't think he wants company right now. In my opinion he ought to be in hospital. He should get checked over. This has been a terrible shock for him. Haven't you got a class to go to?"

"It's PE," Sasha said. "I've got a doctor's note, so I don't have to take part."

"I'd better be going."

Sasha watched her as she headed in the direction of the main building. She waited until the French teacher was inside and walked towards the boy's accommodation block.

* * *

"The only way we're going to get into that car is by breaking a window."

DC Glenda Taylor had checked all four doors on the Audi Q7 and none of them opened the car.

"This is the latest model," her colleague, DC Steve Clough said. "Keyless entry. Push-button start. No doubt it's got a state-of-the-art alarm system too. We break one of the windows on this thing and sirens are going to blare out."

According to the manager at the tennis club Theresa Green's car was parked outside when he arrived for work at eight that morning. O'Reilly and the team back in St Peter Port were still waiting for the security officer to send over the CCTV footage, so there was no way of knowing exactly how long the vehicle had been parked there.

"The windows are tinted," DC Taylor said. "So you can't really see what's inside. We need to get into the car."

"I'll give the boss a call," DC Clough said. "We're going to have to smash a window, but I want DI Peters' say-so before we do that."

The call went straight to voicemail. DC Clough left a short message and rang off.

"What now?" he asked.

"We wait. How much do you reckon these things cost?"

"This is the V12 TDI Limited with all the bells and whistles," DC Clough said. "Easily a hundred grand's worth of car."

DC Taylor let out a whistle. "I paid less than that for my apartment five years ago. There's far too much money on this island."

Her phone started to ring.

She looked at the screen. "It's the boss."

"Glenda," DI Peters said when she'd answered it. "Can you see inside the car?"

"The windows are too dark," she said. "Tinted glass."
"Break it. We have reason to believe Mrs Green has suffered the same fate as her husband, and she could be inside the car."
"We don't really think that, do we, sir?"
"It's highly unlikely," DI Peters confirmed. "But it gives us justification to break into the vehicle."

DC Taylor ended the call and told DC Clough what DI Peters had authorised.
"I'll get the crowbar from the car," DC Clough said. He opened the boot of his Hyundai and retrieved the crowbar.
"Brace yourself," he said as he raised it in the air. "The alarms on these things are like air raid sirens." He took aim and turned his head away. The crowbar shattered the passenger window effortlessly. The two forensics officers waited for the wail of the car alarm but it didn't come.

"That's odd," DC Clough said. "The alarm on the Q7 is automatically activated when the car is locked with the key fob."
"Can you open the doors?" DC Taylor said.
"Not without the fey fob. Technology is a wonderful thing, but sometimes it's a curse. Everything on this vehicle is operated via a central computer system.

We're going to have to pry the doors open the old-fashioned way. Stick your hand in there and find the inside handle. Push the lever up while I get to work with the crowbar."

It took less than five seconds to get the passenger door open. There was a loud crunch and DC Clough opened it wide.

"This ought to confuse the insurance company when Mrs Green submits her claim," he said.

He put on a pair of gloves and took a look inside the Audi. The interior was immaculate.

"Looks like she's just had a full valet done," DC Clough said. "It's like it just came out of the showroom."

"Or perhaps she wanted to clean it for another reason," DC Taylor said. "Getting rid of evidence."

"I don't think she was cleaning away evidence," DC Clough said a minute later.

He'd managed to open up the glove compartment.

"If that was the case," he added. "I don't think she would have left this behind."

He held it up for DC Taylor to see. The paring knife looked extremely sharp. Later if would be confirmed that it was the missing knife from the block inside the kitchen of number 2 Rue La Mere, and it would also be established that the dried blood on the blade came from Arnold Green.

CHAPTER EIGHT

O'Reilly got the call from Steve Clough just after two that afternoon. DC Clough and DC Taylor had found the possible murder weapon in Theresa Green's car, but Mrs Green was still proving to be a difficult woman to track down. They still hadn't received the CCTV footage from the car park, and O'Reilly was starting to get annoyed. That footage could possibly give them the answers they needed. Once they knew when Theresa left the tennis club they would have a definite timeline to work from.

DC Owen came inside O'Reilly's office.
"I got hold of Arnold Green's lawyer, sir," she said. "He was very cooperative."
"That's very refreshing," O'Reilly said. "What do we know?"
"Mr Green's last Will and Testament is rather complicated."
"They always are where the filthy rich are concerned. Is the lawyer willing to send us a copy?"
"No, sir," DC Owen said. "Not without a warrant ordering him to do so. But he has offered to discuss it face to face."
"I think I've seen everything now, Katie. A cooperative lawyer. He must be in a good mood today."
"He's busy with clients most of the day," DC Owen

said. "But he can fit us in after five."

"Then that will have to do."

"Do you think Mrs Green did it?" DC Owen asked. "Do you think she killed her husband?"

"The knife in the glove compartment would suggest it," O'Reilly said. "But something feels off about the whole thing."

"I think so too. It's a little bit too convenient, isn't it? Why would she leave her car parked at the tennis club with the knife inside? It would only be a matter of time before we found the car, and the knife hadn't even been wiped clean. The alarm wasn't activated either, which suggests whoever drove the car to the tennis club didn't drive it very often. This stinks of a set-up."

"It certainly does. This one is already giving me a headache and we've only been at it a couple of hours. A schoolboy announces to the entire class that his father is dead and it was his mother who killed him. Later that day we find the mother's car with the murder weapon inside it."

"Do you think the boy is involved somehow?" DC Owen said.

"I can't see how, Katie. He's been at school the whole day, so if he did kill his dad and plant the knife in the car, how did he get it to the tennis club in Les Martins? We need that CCTV footage."

"It's just come in, sir?"

DC Stone was standing in the doorway.

"And?" O'Reilly asked.

"The car has been at the tennis club all night," DC Stone told him. "According to the footage it arrived there just after three this morning."

"What about the driver?" DC Owen said. "Who was driving it?"

"It's impossible to tell," DC Stone said. "The footage isn't great and whoever left the car there obviously knew about the cameras. You can just make out a figure getting out and making their way across the car park in the direction of Pleinheaume."

"That's on the way back to Vazon," DC Owen pointed out.

"How far is it from Les Martins to Rue La Mare in Vazon?" O'Reilly wondered.

"A couple of miles," DC Stone said. "Three max."

"A doable walk then."

"What are you thinking, sir?" DC Owen said.

"James Green has an alibi for today," O'Reilly said. "He was at school from eight, and he's still there, but we don't know where he was last night. It's possible he killed his father, planted the knife in his mother's car, drove it to Les Martins and walked back home under cover of darkness."

"You can't possibly think a teenage boy did this," DC Stone said.

"I'm just looking at what we know, Andy. James Green had the opportunity to carry it out. His strange behaviour earlier could be the effects of realising what he'd done. That boy is still at the top of the list."

"Are we going to bring him in?" DC Owen said.

"I don't think we have much of a choice, do we? Especially in light of what we know about the timescale. I've got an appointment with Arnold Green's lawyer at five, and if James Green stands to gain from his father's death, we've got a motive. James had opportunity, and I've got a strong feeling he also had a strong reason for wanting his father dead."

"What about the mother?" DC Owen said. "What about Mrs Green? Where does she feature in this? If James stands to gain from his father's death, what about his mother? Surely, she would be first in line to inherit Arnold's fortune."

"I'll find that out when I get a look at the Will," O'Reilly said. "And if James is due to inherit his father's millions, we've got enough to arrest the boy and we've got enough to charge him."

"It still feels too easy, sir," DC Owen said. "Arnold Green was only discovered this morning and we already have a suspect with opportunity and a possible motive. It doesn't feel right. It's too easy."

"It happens, Katie," O'Reilly said. "James Green is a teenage boy. He's not exactly a criminal mastermind. And it's also looking like he's trying to frame his mother. But he hasn't done a very good job of it. We'll make up our mind when I've seen what's in that Will."

"James has a sister, doesn't he?" DC Stone remined them.

"That's right," O'Reilly said. "She's eighteen, she's on holiday somewhere in southeast Asia, and we haven't been able to find her."

"If she's the older sibling, surely she would be first in line to the father's millions."

"We'll wait until we know what's in that Will," O'Reilly said. "I want to have the briefing after that, and then we'll decide on a plan of action. In the meantime, I want the search for Theresa Green moved up a notch. Someone must know where that damn woman is."

CHAPTER NINE

The offices of Brown and Henshaw were only a stone's throw from the station, so O'Reilly decided to walk. He'd informed Stephan Brown that he was on his way and the lawyer had told him he was expecting him. O'Reilly walked at a quicker pace than usual, and his leg was complaining about it. The ache in the bone was getting worse but O'Reilly kept going, nevertheless. He needed to know what was in James Green's Last Will and Testament and he needed to know that now. The contents of that Will were the key to how they were going to move forward in the investigation and O'Reilly's impatience was overruling the discomfort in his femur.

He understood DC Owen's concerns about the simplicity of their discoveries. They were led straight to the body via James Green's bizarre outburst in class. The murder weapon had been discovered a few hours later through some routine detective work, and O'Reilly knew that murder investigations were rarely this simple. He'd been involved in countless murder cases over the years, and he couldn't recall one that had been brought to its conclusion so quickly, but stranger things had happened so he decided to keep an open mind until something changed it.

He pressed the buzzer on the side of the door and soon afterwards a green light appeared on the display to tell him the door was unlocked. He went inside and walked up to the reception desk.

"DI O'Reilly," he told the man sitting there. "I have an appointment with Mr Brown at five."

"Brown senior?" the receptionist asked. "Or Brown junior?"

"Stephan," O'Reilly said.

"Of course. Please take a seat, and I'll inform Mr Brown that you're here."

O'Reilly didn't want to sit down – he wanted some answers. He didn't get the chance anyway. A door in front of him opened before he'd even reached the row of chairs, and a man in his sixties walked up to him. He held out his hand. "Detective O'Reilly, I presume. Stephan Brown. Please follow me."

Brown senior then, O'Reilly decided.

He shook the hand and followed the lawyer down a wide corridor.

They stopped at a black door, Stephan pushed it open and beckoned for O'Reilly to go inside.

"Please take a seat. Can I offer you something to drink?"

"Tea would be grand," O'Reilly said. "If it's not too much trouble."

"I'll ask Diane to arrange it," Stephan said and walked back out.

O'Reilly took in the room. He'd found himself in plenty of lawyers' offices in the past, but this one was very impressive. Everything inside looked old and everything seemed to have a story to tell. The bookcases against two of the walls were teak, and the volumes within seemed well-thumbed. A gigantic desk stood almost in the middle of the room and O'Reilly was surprised to see the number of photographs on it. The frames were silver and all of them depicted family members in various parts of the island. Stephan Brown was clearly a family man. The huge window behind the desk offered a panoramic view of Belle Greve Bay. It was a clear day, and the island of Herm was visible in the distance.

Stephan came back with a tray of tea. He placed it on the desk in front of O'Reilly.

"Help yourself. It's not a bad view, is it? I had to position the desk so I had my back to it. Otherwise, I very much doubt I'd ever get any work done."

O'Reilly poured himself some tea. "Can I pour you one too?"

"No, thank you. I only drink coffee, and I only allow myself two cups in the morning. Shall we get straight down to business?"

"I need to take a look at Arnold Green's Last Will and Testament," O'Reilly said.

"Of course," Stephan said. "Tragic business. Are you any closer to discovering the truth about what happened?"

"It's still early days. Right now, we're just going through the motions."

"I see. And murder for money is always at the top of the list, isn't it?"

"You'd be surprised."

"Are you investigating Theresa?"

"What makes you say that?" O'Reilly said.

"Simple assumption. If Arnold's murder was about his money, it's logical to think you'd be most interested in the person who stands to gain the most from his death."

"And that would be Mrs Green?"

Stephan opened up a thick file on the desk. "Is that it?" O'Reilly asked. "Is that Mr Green's Will?"

"It is," Stephan confirmed. "And I'm sure you're aware that the contents within are bound by attorney-client privilege. I'm not obliged to share what I'm about to reveal, but I'm giving you some of the details out of common courtesy to a law I hold in high regard."

"I appreciate that."

"Mr Green's final wishes are of a rather complicated nature, so I'll give you the general gist of it, shall I?"

"I'd appreciate that too," O'Reilly said.

"Arnold Green had assets amounting to roughly thirty-eight million pounds," Stephan said. "I won't bore you with the ins and outs of how these assets are comprised. Upon his death, the majority of the estate has been bequeathed to his wife, Theresa."

"How much of a majority are we talking about?"

"Roughly seventy percent. The balance is to be split equally between the two children."

O'Reilly wasn't particularly good at Maths but after a quick calculation he figured out that James and his sister would inherit roughly five million pounds each."

"There are conditions of course," Stephan carried on. "Obviously, should there be a dissolution of the marriage, a special clause would take effect."

"What's in the special clause?" O'Reilly asked.

"Then the entire estate would be split between the children."

"Mr Green was estranged from his wife, wasn't he?" O'Reilly said. "Do you know if he was planning on filing for divorce?"

"It was never mentioned."

"I suppose Mrs Green would still come out alright if they did get divorced," O'Reilly said. "She would still get half of what he owns."

"Absolutely not," Stephan said. "In the event of a divorce Mrs Green wouldn't receive a penny. The pre-nuptial contract makes sure of that."

"She signed a pre-nup?"

"I've already told you too much, but yes. She was left with little choice. Rudolph insisted on it. Rudolph was Arnold's father and he stipulated precisely that when he drafted his own Last Will and Testament."

"I'm starting to get a bit behind here," O'Reilly admitted. "Are you telling me Arnold's father made it a condition in his Will that Arnold wouldn't get a cent if he didn't have a pre-nuptial contract with Theresa stating she couldn't get her hands on the cash in the event of a divorce."

"That's about the size of it. It's not uncommon. There are more unscrupulous women out there than we think. The Greens are a respectable family on the island. They've earned their money through hard graft and shrewd business decisions, and Rudolph wasn't about to see that wealth taken away by a money-grabbing hussy. His words. Rudolph was a peculiar man."

"Have you known the Greens long?" O'Reilly said.
"I knew Rudolph well," Stephan said. "And I've known Arnold since he was a boy."
"What about the children?"
"I've met them on occasion. James and Vanessa seem to have their heads screwed on."
"We're trying to find Vanessa," O'Reilly said. "She's travelling somewhere in southeast Asia, and we haven't been able to locate her."
"I'm afraid I can't help you there."
"Surely, you'll need to get in touch with her to discuss her father's death?"
"That's correct, but that has nothing to do with your investigation."
"I'd appreciate it if you'd keep me informed," O'Reilly said. "We really need to talk to her."
"I'll see what I can do. Will there be anything else? I promised my wife I wouldn't be too late home. It's her sister's birthday and we were planning on going out."
"Just one more question," O'Reilly said. "The Green kids are set to inherit ten million between them. Surely they're a bit young to handle that kind of responsibility. There must be some kind of age thing

specified in the Will."

"There is," Stephan said. "And it was something Arnold and I firmly disagreed upon when he asked me to draft the Will."

"You advised him not to leave them so much?" O'Reilly speculated.

"It wasn't the amount that we argued about. In my experience when substantial wealth is involved, I suggest to my clients that the funds be placed in an interest-bearing trust until such an age that the beneficiaries are responsible enough to take ownership of it. Twenty-five is what I usually put forward. Any earlier than that and there is the risk of the money being squandered carelessly."

"But Arnold Green didn't agree?" O'Reily said.

"Unfortunately, not," Stephan said. "And I was in no position to go against his wishes. He insisted that upon his death James and Vanessa will inherit their share when they reach the age of eighteen. Vanessa had already reached that age and James has just over a year to go before he inherits what's due to him."

CHAPTER TEN

"As things stand," O'Reilly addressed the team in the briefing room. "If we look at Arnold Green's murder from the perspective of killing for money, we have three possible suspects."

The conversation with Stephan Brown had given him a few things to think about. In the event of Arnold's death his wife and his two children stood to benefit considerably. Theresa would inherit the lion's share, but James and Vanessa would also come into a substantial amount of money. Vanessa would get hers as soon as the nitty gritty was sorted out and James would receive his share on the day of his eighteenth birthday.

O'Reilly told the team as much.

"Mr Green's lawyer explained that his client's decision was a very unusual one," he added. "Eighteen is a very young age to inherit that kind of money, but Arnold was insistent. Those kids are going to be very well off indeed."

"Five million each?" DC Stone said. "When I was eighteen I had about twelve quid in the bank."

"Vanessa Green is blissfully unaware she's probably the richest kid in southeast Asia right now," O'Reilly said. "Stephan Brown has promised to let me know if he manages to contact her, but unless she phones home, it's going to be difficult."

"I hope she doesn't have to find out from social media," DC Owen said. "That's not the nicest way to discover your father has been murdered."

"You said she was a suspect?" DS Skinner said. "How can she be a suspect when she's thousands of miles away?"

"Until we know exactly where she is," O'Reilly said. "We're treating her as a suspect. She stands to gain substantially from her father's death, as do her brother and her mother. Mrs Green's whereabouts still remain a mystery, so we'll concentrate on James."

"I can't believe a sixteen-year-old would kill his dad just to get his hands on his money," DS Skinner said. "It doesn't make sense. James will never have to want for anything in his life. He goes to the best school – he probably takes exotic holidays, and he lives in a house none of us will ever be able to afford. Why murder the man who provided all that for him?"

"I agree with the DS," DC Stone said. "Five million might sound a lot to the likes of us, but it's small change for a spoilt rich kid."

"He's still our main suspect," O'Reilly insisted.

"Are we going to arrest him?" DC Owen asked.

O'Reilly nodded. "We are, Katie. His father's lawyer pressed me about it as I was leaving. I didn't give too much away, but Stephan Brown is a sharp cookie, and he knows the score. I've got a feeling that this is going to be complicated. Given James's age we're going to have our work cut out getting through the legal red tape Brown and Henshaw are no doubt going to throw at us."

"We've got a rough time of death for Arnold Green," DS Skinner said. "According to Dr Lille he was killed sometime between two and four this morning."

"We can narrow it down further," O'Reilly said. "Once forensics confirm the knife found in Theresa Green's car is the murder weapon, we can safely knock at least an hour off that time. The car the knife was in arrived at the tennis club just after three. It's not a long drive from Vazon, but whoever drove the car would still have had to place the knife in the glove compartment and drive over to Les Martins. They would have had to do this after stabbing a man over a dozen times, so they probably would have got blood on them. There was no blood found in the vehicle so whoever drove to the tennis club cleaned themselves up first."

"James Green is only sixteen," DC Stone said. "He's not old enough to drive."

"If James is our killer," O'Reilly said. "I very much doubt he'd be concerned about driving without a license."

"That wasn't what I meant, sir. How does he even

know how to drive a car in the first place?"

"Rich kids don't live in the same world as us, Andy," DC Owen said. "His dad will probably have let him drive from an early age. And Theresa Green's Q7 is the automatic model. It's not a difficult vehicle to drive."

"Plus there will have been very few cars on the road at that time in the morning," DS Skinner pointed out.

"He's a suspect," O'Reilly said. "He had the opportunity, and he has a strong motive."

"How are we going to play it?" DC Stone asked. "He's still at Vazon High. Are we going to storm the place and drag him back here?"

"Hold your horses," O'Reilly said. "That is what we're definitely *not* going to do. The press will have already got wind of what's happened, and if I know Fred Viking, he'll have one of his vultures camped out close to the school. We have to do this carefully."

"Why? Because he's a rich kid?"

"Asked and answered, Andy," O'Reilly said. "It stinks but that's just how it works in a place like Guernsey."

"It's still not right."

"We can argue until we're blue in the face about the inequality in the world," O'Reilly said. "It's a fruitless indaba. It is what it is, and the fact of the matter is, we have to do things differently."

"Put it past the Chief first?" DC Owen guessed.

"Got it in one, Katie. But seeing as the big boss is in Paris right now, the Deputy Chief Officer will have to do. DCO Dove and me have an understanding – the man owes me a few favours."

"What's the story with you and the DCO?" DC Stone said.

O'Reilly's first encounter with the deputy chief officer had been a rather strange one. DCO Callum Dove had been crossing the road while staring at the screen of his mobile phone. O'Reilly had pushed him out of the way of an oncoming car. The BMW wasn't travelling very fast, and it was unlikely the DCO would have been badly injured but it could have been very embarrassing for him if there had been an accident. The man who was second in charge of the Island Police had asked O'Reilly to keep the incident quiet and the Irishman had obliged. But an unspoken agreement had come out of it, and O'Reilly was planning on abusing the terms of that agreement again.

"It's a long story, Andy," he told DC Stone. "And we haven't got time for long stories right now. Let's just say we'll have James Green in an interview room within the hour."

He got up and reached for his stick, then remembered he'd left it in his office.

"Do you want me to go and fetch it?" DC Stone offered.

"Thanks, but no thanks. I think it's time I ditched the damn thing and started to walk without it. I'll be five minutes with the DCO, and we'll be good to go."

He left the briefing room and made his way to the staircase that led upstairs to the offices of the men and women who called the shots. He didn't even make it halfway.

"Sir." It was PC London.

"What is it, Kim?" O'Reilly asked her.

"We've got another dead man."

"Go on."

"His name is John Hillman," PC London said. "His daughter came home from school and found him."

"What do we know?"

"Looks like he was attacked with a golf club," PC London said. "There was a golf bag in the hallway. But I think you should know this – his daughter goes to the same school as James Green."

"Interesting," O'Reilly said.

"That's not all. The address the girl gave was number 4 Rue La Mere. The dead man lives in the house next door to Arnold Green."

CHAPTER ELEVEN

O'Reilly made the decision to head straight to Rue La Mere. James Green could wait. The teenage boy wasn't going anywhere, and it would probably be better to pick him up in the morning anyway. He got a lift with DCI Fish. The DCI had arrived at the station just as O'Reilly was ready to leave. O'Reilly had been surprised to see him but when DCI Fish explained that Superintendent Hayes had told him he was needed at work, it didn't take O'Reilly long to understand what was happening.

"Not long now, Tom," he said.
They'd just passed Le Foulon and they were heading west towards Vazon.
"Soon there'll be a little human being in your lives," O'Reilly added.
"Between you and me," DCI Fish said. "I'm counting down the days. Anne is driving me nuts. I think it's the hormones. It's clear she needs help, but when I offer assistance all I get is abuse."

A smile started to form on O'Reilly's face. He managed to control it before it became too obvious.

"Women," he offered. "Don't even try to figure them out."

"Take this morning for example," DCI Fish hadn't finished yet. "We've been putting the finishing touches to the nursery. I was about to make a start on hanging up a mobile I made. It has a school of silver fish on it, and I thought it rather apt. Fish for the little fish. Anne took one look at it and begged me to make her a cup of tea. She said she was craving a cup of tea, and she needed it now."

"They do crave funny things," O'Reilly said.

"Well, I made the tea and when I came back to the room, the mobile was on the floor in pieces. Anne apologised and said she'd accidentally sat on it. It was ruined."

"Accidents happen," O'Reilly said.

The smile was refusing to budge now.

"And when I looked up, I noticed another mobile had been pinned up in its place. It was a whole load of teddy bears. Anne must have put it there while I was making the tea. I give up, I really do."

The flashing lights of police cars could be seen in the distance and O'Reilly was glad. He wasn't sure how long he would be able to stop himself from erupting into fits of laughter. As they got closer, he spotted an ambulance and a number of other vehicles he recognised. Forensics were already here.

It was when DCI Fish had parked the car and he and O'Reilly had got out that he spotted a vehicle that didn't belong there. It was the van belonging to the Island Herald. O'Reilly shouldn't have been surprised – the noses of the staff employed by Fred *the Ed* Viking were notorious for their ability to sniff out a juicy scoop. He spotted the main man himself after he'd crossed the road. Fred Viking was talking to another man behind the van. O'Reilly didn't recognise him.

"Give me a second," he said to DCI Fish.

"What's wrong?"

"I just need to speak to someone."

DCI Fish spotted the Herald's van.

"Don't do anything stupid, Liam."

"I wouldn't dream of it," O'Reilly assured him. "I just want to have a quick chat."

Fred Viking spotted O'Reilly when he was ten metres away. The editor of The Herald nodded his head in greeting.

"You need to leave," O'Reilly informed him.

"The last time I checked," Fred said. "The Bailiwick of Guernsey was a free island. As a tax paying resident,

I'm at liberty to wander as I see fit."

"This is a crime scene, Viking. Get lost."

"When measures are put in place to inform us of such," his friend said. "We will gladly vacate the scene. I don't see anything to suggest a crime has been committed here. No police tape, officers waving flags etc."

"And who might you be?" O'Reilly asked him.

"Lewis Michaels."

He held out his hand. O'Reilly observed it as though it was a steaming dog turd.

"He's just joined us," Fred explained. "He's Eric's replacement."

"Eric Rivers has been dead for months," O'Reilly reminded him.

"And someone of his calibre isn't easily replaced. But I have every confidence in Lewis's abilities."

    O'Reilly knew he was wasting his time bickering with a man for whom bickering was considered a hobby. He left them to it and started to walk back towards DCI Fish.

"O'Reilly," Fred called after him. "We've got something nasty here, haven't we? The headlines are already taking form in my head."

O'Reilly turned around. "Piss off, Viking."

"You'll like this one," Fred said. "What do you think of *Murders on the Rue Morgue*? Or are you not familiar with Poe?"

O'Reilly knew who Edgar Allen Poe was, and as much as he hated to admit it, Fred Viking's idea for a headline really was quite catchy. He put the repulsive thought out of his head.

"What do we know so far?" he asked DCI Fish outside number 4 Rue La Mare.

"The deceased is John Hillman. Forty-one years' old. His sixteen-year-old daughter came home from school and found him in the hallway."

"She attends the same school as the son of the man found dead next door," O'Reilly told him. "Vazon High. That is not a coincidence."

"Let's not jump to conclusions, Liam."

"I'm not buying it, Tom. We have two dead men. Two men who live next door to one another, who also happen to have offspring who attend the same prestigious school. We cannot ignore that."

He looked at the house. It was very similar to number 2 in design. Even though the houses could be considered to be *next-door* there was quite a distance between the two. O'Reilly estimated the gap between the properties to be around twenty metres. This wasn't the kind of neighbourhood where cups of sugar were passed across the fence to your next-door-neighbour. He wondered whether the two victims even knew each other. He reckoned they would have done. Their children went to the same school. They were acquainted, and he was convinced there was something else that linked the two men. There was some other connection that resulted in both of them being murdered within hours of each other.

"What are you thinking?" DCI Fish said.
"When have you ever been involved in a murder where the victims lived next door to one another?"
"It's not common."
"It's unheard of," O'Reilly said. "This isn't a big island, but even so, the odds on two people being murdered on the same street are astronomical. And the odds of them being dispatched within hours of each other doesn't even bear thinking about. There is a connection here on this street."

The paramedics were twiddling their thumbs next to the ambulance and this told O'Reilly that DI Peters was still busy with the body inside. Something occurred to him.
"Where's the girl?" he asked DCI Fish.

"I don't know."

"I want to speak to her," O'Reilly said and walked up to the house.

The PCs Hill and Woodbine were standing sentry by the gate.

"Greg," O'Reilly said to PC Hill. "What happened to the girl who found the body?"

"I'm not sure, sir," PC Hill said.

"I think she went next door," PC Woodbine said.

"You think?" O'Reilly asked the man mountain of a PC. "Find out where she is. I need to talk to her."

PC Woodbine marched off to number 6.

"What's going on here, sir?" PC Hill said.

"Something we haven't considered yet," O'Reilly said. "Two men living next door to each other have been killed in the space of a few hours and I don't like it. What do we know about the dead man?"

"Just his name right now. John Hillman. His daughter, Sasha came home from school and found him. Looks like he was beaten to death with a golf club."

"What about the mother? Where is she?"

"I don't know, sir."

"There's too much we don't know right now," O'Reilly said. "I need to talk to that girl."

PC Woodbine returned. There was no sign of Sasha Hillman.

"Where is she?" O'Reilly asked.

"She's gone, sir," PC Woodbine told him.

"What do you mean she's gone? I thought you said she was next door."

"I thought she was, but the couple who live at number 6 said she left."

"This is just fekkin brilliant."

O'Reilly left them to think about this, and made his way next door. The lights were on downstairs and O'Reilly caught a glimpse of someone peeking out behind the curtains in the living room. He walked up the path to the front door and rang the bell. The door was opened shortly afterwards by a man who looked to be in his late fifties. A tall woman of similar age was standing behind him.

O'Reilly took out his ID. "DI O'Reilly, Island Police. Can I come in?"

"We've already spoken to the men in uniform," the man informed him.

"I just need to ask you a few questions."

"I'll put the kettle on," the woman said.

"You'd better come in then."

The man introduced himself as Benjamin Dodds and his wife was Jane. He led O'Reilly to a large living room and asked him to take a seat.

"Where did Sasha go?" O'Reilly came straight to the point.

"I don't know," Benjamin said. "She said she needed the bathroom, and she didn't come back."

"Did you hear her leave?"

"I didn't hear anything. I just assumed she'd gone up to the bathroom."

"The place is swarming with police," O'Reilly said. "How did she manage to slip away?"

"She must have gone out the back. There's a gate in the back garden that opens onto the nature reserve. Perhaps she went out that way."

"Show me."

Benjamin stood up and left the room. O'Reilly followed him down the hallway. The back door was in the kitchen, and it was wide open.

"I'll switch on the lights," Benjamin said.

He flicked a switch and the back garden lit up. A swimming pool glimmered blue off to the left.

"The gate is down here," Benjamin said and started to walk through the garden.

O'Reilly caught up with him halfway down. The entire garden was surrounded with a six-foot fence and the gate was located behind an old oak tree. Beyond that was the rolling fields of the St Germain Nature Reserve.

"Is the gate kept locked?" O'Reilly asked.

"We didn't think it was necessary," Benjamin replied.

"You're not concerned about security?"

"We've had no problems in the past. Besides, we've got the security beams and the CCTV cameras. This is a safe area."

Until two men were murdered on the same street, O'Reily thought.

He kept this to himself.

"When did you last see Sasha?" he said.

"Probably about twenty minutes ago," Benjamin said. "She could be anywhere by now then. Why did she up and leave?"

"I had no idea she was planning on doing that."

"How did she seem to you?"

"She was probably in shock," Benjamin said. "She's just come home and found her father beaten to death. Perhaps she wasn't thinking straight when she left, or maybe she needed to be on her own. Why are you so keen to talk to her?"

O'Reilly sighed deeply. "Never mind. If she does come back, give me a call."

He handed Benjamin one of his cards.

"Straight away," he added.

CHAPTER TWELVE

O'Reilly looked at his watch. It was almost eight, and he decided to call it a day. Jim Peters and the rest of the forensics team were still busy with both number 2 and number 4 Rue La Mere, and Sasha Hillman still hadn't turned up. He'd found a photograph of the Year 11 girl, and every available police officer was keeping an eye out for her. There wasn't much more O'Reilly could do tonight. He would interview James Green in the morning, and he wasn't looking forward to it. James would no doubt come with reinforcements and O'Reilly knew from bitter experience that when that happened it inevitably slowed down the progress of an investigation. James's mother, Theresa was also proving to be a difficult woman to find. There had been no sightings of her all day and O'Reilly was starting to wonder if she was even still on the island.

He tried to put the series of events into some kind of order. James Green had told the entire class that he'd found the body of his father before he left for school that morning. Dr Lille put the time of death somewhere between two and four in the morning, but CCTV had confirmed that Theresa Green's vehicle had arrived at the tennis club around three. The car contained the murder weapon, so it was safe to assume that whoever was driving it was responsible for killing Arnold Green.

"CCTV," O'Reilly told the window in his office. When he'd spoken to the couple at number 6 Rue La Mere earlier Benjamin Dodds had told him the house was secure because of the security beams and the CCTV cameras.

O'Reilly found his phone and dialled DI Peters' number.

The Head of Forensics picked up straight away.

"Jim," O'Reilly said. "Any developments?"

"We've still got a lot to go through," DI Peters said. "It looks like the killer attacked Mr Hillman and got out of the house straight away. The only evidence of a struggle was in the vicinity of the body."

"Any sign of the murder weapon?"

"The 9 iron was missing from the golf set. I'm ninety-nine percent certain that's what was used. We've searched the whole house, but it looks like he took it with him after killing Mr Hillman. A golf club would be relatively easy to hide under a coat."

"Can I ask you to speak to one of the neighbours?" O'Reilly got to the point of the phone call. "Benjamin Dodds at number 6. We spoke to him earlier and he told us he has CCTV cameras."

"You're wondering if they might have caught the killer making his getaway?"

"Exactly. We might get lucky. Mrs Green's Audi was found at the tennis club in Les Martins so the driver would probably have passed number 6 on the way, and it's possible whoever killed John Hillman got caught on camera too."

"I'll send Henry over there," DI Peters said.

"I appreciate it," O'Reilly told him. "I'm knocking off for the day, but I've got my mobile phone on."

"I'll let you know if we get anything from the CCTV footage."

They said their goodbyes and O'Reilly stood up to leave. A twinge in his leg caused him to wince. It was an unfamiliar ache, and he didn't know what was causing it. He picked up his stick and hobbled out of the office. The pain in his leg was getting worse – it was a persistent ache that intensified each time he put his weight on the gammy leg. O'Reilly recalled the brisk walk to the lawyers' offices, and he made a mental note not to do that again. It was still early days and he had quite a way to go before his leg was back to how it used to be.

DC Stone was lingering by the front desk when O'Reilly emerged from the corridor and the Irish detective was glad. He needed a lift home, and he knew the rat-faced man would be happy to oblige. He informed him as much.

"No problem, sir," DC Stone said. "Is the leg giving you problems?"

"I think I've pushed it a bit too far today, Andy," O'Reilly said. "Are you ready to go?"

* * *

"I'm scared."

Sasha Hillman had seen better days. Her fair skin was blotchy in places and her eyes were red and puffy. Her blond hair was a mess of rat's tails, and her clothes were crumpled and dirty. She was still wearing her school uniform, and there was a rip in the sleeve of her blouse from when she snagged it in the thick brambles at the end of the garden of number 6 Rue La Mere. All in all, she'd definitely looked better. James Green still thought she was the most beautiful girl he'd ever seen.

"You don't have to be scared," he told her. "I won't let anything happen to you."

He pulled her closer to him and brushed a stray strand of hair away from her eyes. She smiled a half-smile, but it didn't quite reach those eyes.

"What's going to happen to us?" Sasha wondered.

"We'll be fine," James promised. "We will always be fine."

"The police are going to come looking for us."

"What of it? My dad's lawyer said I'm going to be questioned tomorrow, but he told me not to worry. I don't have to talk to them if I don't want to, and because of my age they're not allowed to lock me up."

"Do you think they know what happened?"

"No," James said. "There's no way they can possibly know. None of this can be linked back to us. We just have to wait it out."

"Can I stay here with you tonight?"

"Do you even have to ask that? We have to be careful though. One of the teachers might come and check up on me, so we have to be careful."

CHAPTER THIRTEEN

O'Reilly turned the key in the lock, but nothing happened. The door wasn't locked. He made his way inside his apartment and the reason for the unlocked door was in the kitchen.

"I hope you don't mind," Assumpta said. "But I felt like a chat, and I let myself in."

"That's why I gave you a key, Summi," O'Reilly told her. "Is there something on your mind?"

A half-full glass of wine stood on the kitchen table. The bottle was next to it.

"Can I get you a beer?" Assumpta asked.

"I'd better not," O'Reilly said. "The leg is giving me grief and I was planning on taking a couple of pain tablets later. I'll make some tea."

He switched on the kettle and put a teabag in a mug. He spooned two sugars in and turned to face his daughter.

"What's up, Summi?"

"Andy has asked me to move in with him."

O'Reilly nodded. "I see. And you're wondering what I think about that?"

"I've got a fairly good idea. I know you don't think he's the right one for me."

"Aside from the fact that he's a spectacularly unattractive man," O'Reilly said. "And he possesses all the attributes of a rodent, what makes you think I don't approve?"

Assumpta finished the wine in the glass and topped it up again.

"Why is your leg giving you trouble?"

"It's nothing I can't fix," O'Reilly said. "Where's the car? I didn't see it parked outside."

He'd let Assumpta use his car while he was still not allowed to drive it.

"I walked here," she said. "My place is only around the corner."

"What is it you want me to tell you, Summi? You're a grown woman, and you don't need my permission."

"It would be nice to have your approval, Dad,"

Assumpta said. "Or at least some semblance of approval. I know you've got your misgivings about Andy, but you don't know him like I do. You only see what he's like at work, but there's a lot more to him than that."

"I suppose I haven't really bothered to look beneath the outer layers," O'Reilly admitted. "But you have to admit what you see on the surface doesn't exactly inspire much."

"He's not that bad looking."

"Hmm," O'Reilly said. "If you want to know the truth, he's actually growing on me. He has the odd moment of real insight and I think if he put his mind to it, he could turn into an exceptional detective. Where exactly is this going? Has he spoken of marriage?"

"Of course not. What makes you say that?"

"It's the next logical step. You move in together, get married and have children. That's how it usually works, isn't it?"

"Well, he hasn't asked me to marry him."

O'Reilly had forgotten about the tea. He didn't feel like one now anyway. He limped over to the fridge and took out a beer. He opened it and took a long drink. Bram and Juliet made an appearance. The ginger tom and the slender black lady were always joined at the hip. They never went anywhere without each other.

Assumpta bent down and scratched Bram's neck. "He's getting fat."

"Bram has always been fat," O'Reilly said. "I really don't know what Juliet sees in him. It must be his riveting personality. I suppose opposites do seem to attract."

He grinned at his daughter.

"Don't say it, Dad," Assumpta warned. "What's really wrong with your leg?"

"I overdid it a bit today. I really needed to talk to the lawyer of one of the dead men and I almost ran to his practice. I won't be doing that again in a hurry."

"What's the story there?" Assumpta asked.

"Off the record?"

"Come on, Dad."

"Off the record," O'Reilly said. "We've got two dead men who just happen to live next door to each other. The kids go to the same school, and I haven't the foggiest idea what's going on."

"Have you seen the latest posts on the Herald's online thing?"

"I don't read Viking's shite," O'Reilly reminded her.

"He's really milking the next-door-neighbour angle."

"He mentioned something about Murders on the Rue Morgue."

"He's taken it further than that," Assumpta said.

She picked up her tablet and swiped the screen. She showed it to O'Reilly.

"Death Rue," he read. "Very inventive. I assume the Gazette is going with something more subtle."

"Fiona's worried about the ratings again," Assumpta said. "You know what she's like."

"She's an editor with integrity. That's what she is."

"Integrity doesn't equate to ratings," Assumpta said. "Integrity doesn't keep the advertisers happy. The Herald is way ahead and none of us have any idea how to catch up."

O'Reilly finished his beer and got himself another. "I might have something for you."

"Really?" Assumpta seemed surprised.

"How much does the Herald know?"

"Arnold Green was killed sometime this morning," Assumpta said. "And John Hillman was murdered later in the day. They also mentioned that it was the kids who found the bodies."

"Where does Viking get his info from?" O'Reilly wondered.

"You know what he's like. He's got a nose like a bloodhound, and he has eyes and ears everywhere."

"Did the Herald post mention anything about the knife that killed Arnold Green being found in his wife's car?" O'Reilly knew immediately that he shouldn't have said that. If it came to light that a detective with the Island Police had divulged this kind of information to the press, there could be serious consequences.

"Is she in custody?" Assumpta asked.

"She would be if we could find her," O'Reilly said. "She's disappeared off the face of the earth."

A smile started to form on Assumpta's face.

"I don't like that grin, Summi," O'Reilly told her. "You're plotting something, aren't you?"

"I think we've got our angle. Mrs Green is missing. Fred Viking doesn't appear to know that. We get a scoop, and we help the Island Police into the bargain."

"How do you figure that out?"

"A public appeal," Assumpta explained. "It's worked in the past. We put out a story about the missing woman and you get every pair of eyes on the island out looking for her."

O'Reilly's phone started to ring before he got the chance to ponder this. The number on the screen told him it was work.

"O'Reilly," he answered it.

"Sir." It was PC Hill. "Sorry to bother you so late, but I thought you'd want to know this."

"What is it, Greg?"

Assumpta couldn't hear the conversation but judging by the expression on her father's face she could tell that something had happened. The call lasted less than a minute. O'Reilly thanked PC Hill and hung up. He took a long swig of his beer.

"Scratch the idea of an appeal," he said to Assumpta.

"What's going on?" she said.

"Theresa Green has been found. She walked into the station fifteen minutes ago."

CHAPTER FOURTEEN

PC Hill informed O'Reilly that Theresa Green had come straight to the Island Police HQ in St Peter Port as soon as she'd heard about the murder of her estranged husband. She claimed she'd spent the night anchored off the island of Herm and her phone battery had died. She only realised she was possibly the most wanted person on Guernsey when she'd sailed back to the island and berthed in the yacht club. The manager of the club had informed her, and she'd made her way straight to the police station.

Assumpta had insisted on driving O'Reilly there – she'd gone home to fetch the car, but he'd been equally insistent when she offered to wait for him. He'd told her to go home – he would get a taxi back to his apartment when he was finished.

"Where is she?" he asked PC Hill.

"She's in one of the interview rooms," PC Hill said. "I didn't know where we stood with her, so I thought I'd wait for you to arrive. Is she going to be arrested?"

"She's the number one suspect in a murder enquiry, Greg. But the fact that she came here of her own volition doesn't feel right. I'll make up my mind when I've had a chat with her. Has she asked for a solicitor?"

"She didn't mention anything," PC Hill said. "She just came in and explained who she was. Said she'd taken the yacht across to Herm last night and only got back to the island late today. Her phone battery had died, and she was oblivious to the fact that we've been looking for her."

"How did she seem to you?"

"Very calm. Rather cold, to be honest. She came in, bold as brass and said she believes her husband has been killed and she's suspected of his murder. She said she came here because that isn't the case."

"Interesting," O'Reilly said. "We need to do this by the book. Is there anyone else to cover the front desk?"

"Sergeant Gough is on duty."

"Grand. I'll ask him to man the desk while we talk to Mrs Green."

"You want me in on the interview?" PC Hill said.

"It's just a formality," O'Reilly explained. "I'll do the talking."

Theresa Green didn't look like a woman suspected of the murder of her husband. She was sitting with her arms folded when O'Reilly and PC Hill came inside the interview room. O'Reilly guessed her age to be somewhere in the mid-thirties. She was very tanned with sun bleached blond hair. She was dressed in a pair of shorts and a T-Shirt and O'Reilly deduced she'd come straight to the station from the marina.

PC Hill started the tape and O'Reilly went through the motions for the record. He asked Theresa if she was sure about not wanting legal representation and she told him it wasn't necessary. She declined his offer of something to drink.

"I just want to get this mess cleared up," she said. Her accent was strange. O'Reilly thought he detected a hint of northern English in there.

"Let's get started then," he said. "I'm very sorry about your husband."

"I'm not."

O'Reilly wasn't expecting this.

"Your husband was brutally murdered this morning," he said. "Your son was the one who found him."

"Where is James?"

"The school were kind enough to offer him a room," O'Reilly said. "We couldn't locate you, and obviously he couldn't stay at home."

"I see. I must give him a call. Is he alright?"

"He's understandably distraught, Mrs Green. He found his father stabbed to death this morning. Arnold sustained over a dozen wounds to his chest, neck and face."

"James will get over it."

"You told PC Hill that you spent the night moored over in Herm," O'Reilly said. "Is that correct?"

Theresa nodded.

"For the tape, Mrs Green is nodding her head. Were you there the whole night?"

"That's right," Theresa said.

"You also said the battery on your phone died, and that's why you didn't know what had happened to Arnold. Is this also correct?"

"I forgot to charge it," Theresa said.

"Isn't that a bit foolhardy? Surely when you're sailing single-handed you should have a means of contacting somebody."

"I have the VHF radio on board," Theresa told him. "And Herm is hardly on the other side of the world. It's only an hour's hop across the bay."

"OK," O'Reilly said. "Is there anyone who can confirm you were on Herm the whole night?"

"I don't think so."

"You didn't speak to anyone over there?"

"I like to be alone," Theresa said. "Single-handed sailing is extremely calming, and when I anchor up, I like to savour the solitude for as long as possible. I crack open a bottle of wine and watch the sun going down over Guernsey. It's very soul warming. You ought to give it a try."

"So, nobody can confirm you were actually across the way on Herm?"

"I told you," Theresa said. "I was alone. How long are you going to keep me here?"

"That depends on whether I get the answers I'm looking for. Perhaps you should reconsider and get in touch with a solicitor."

"Am I under arrest?"

"Not yet," O'Reilly said.

"Can I at least use the bathroom?" Theresa asked. "I wasn't expecting this to take so long."

"Of course," O'Reilly said. "PC Hill will escort you."

He paused the tape and asked PC Hill to organise some tea while he was at it.

CHAPTER FIFTEEN

O'Reilly wasn't sure what to think. Theresa Green had come to the station voluntarily and she hadn't come across as someone who'd recently stabbed her estranged husband more than a dozen times. She was extremely unruffled by the situation, and she didn't seem remotely perturbed about the brutal murder of the father of her children. Something didn't feel right. Theresa Green was either an extremely cold individual or she hadn't yet grasped the severity of what had happened.

She came back into the interview room with PC Hill. The young PC placed a tray of tea on the table and sat down.

"Thanks, Greg," O'Reilly said. "Mrs Green, can I pour you a cup?"

"I don't want tea," Theresa said. "I want to get out of here."

O'Reilly restarted the tape and resumed the interview.

"You own a blue Audi Q6," he said. "Is that correct?"

"Q7," Theresa corrected.

"When was the last time you drove that vehicle?"

"Probably about a week ago."

"You told us you sailed out of the marina here in the capital yesterday," O'Reilly said. "Your house is in

Vazon. How did you get to the yacht club?"

"In the BMW."

"You have another car?"

"It's a nippy little two-seater," Theresa elaborated. "I use it to pop out to the shops. It's a much easier car to park than the Q7. I bought that when the kids were younger. But I rarely drive it these days."

"And you drove the BMW to the yacht club?"

"I just told you I did."

O'Reilly decided on a change of tack.

"You don't live with your husband any longer. Is that correct?"

"It is."

"Can you explain what he was doing at the house on Rue La Mere last night?"

"I really have no idea," Theresa said. "Is this going to take much longer?"

"That's up to you," O'Reilly said. "Can you think of any reason why Arnold would be at your house last night?"

"I don't know why he was there."

"Does he still have a key to the house?" O'Reilly said.

"He moved out two months ago," Theresa said. "I told him to leave, and he left. I insisted he leave his keys behind."

"Why did you ask him to leave?"

"That's none of your business."

"It's very much my business," O'Reilly argued. "Please answer the question."

"I couldn't stand the sight of him anymore. I told him to fuck off and move in with his tart."

"Mr Green was having an affair?"

"Do I have to spell it out for you?"

"That won't be necessary," O'Reilly said. "I believe Mr Green's family were extremely rich."

"What's that got to do with anything?"

"And I also understand that in the event of a divorce you will receive nothing. Is that correct?"

He received a shrug of the shoulders by way of a reply.

"Please answer the question," he urged. "Is it not true that when you and Arnold were married his father insisted on a pre-nuptial contract being in place?"

"He was an even bigger bastard than Arnold."

"I'll take that as a yes then?" O'Reilly said. "Should you and Arnold ever divorce, you won't be entitled to any of his assets?"

"That's right."

"But," O'Reilly said. "And this is what's niggling away at me, there is no such stipulation in the event of Arnold's death. You will inherit almost everything. Am

I right?"

"You think you're so clever, don't you?" Theresa said.

"I assure you I don't," O'Reilly said. "But you can see how this looks from where I'm sitting. Your husband was having an affair, so you kick him out. That's all very well, but what happens next? The logical next step is divorce, and you would come out with nothing if that happened. So, you see only one way out. For you to get your hands on Arnold's money he has to be dead."

"You are so far off the mark it isn't even funny," Theresa said.

"I'm not laughing."

His phone started to ring in his pocket. He'd forgotten to put it on silent. He turned it off and sighed deeply.

"Mrs Green," he said. "Theresa, I'm afraid things aren't looking good for you. You have a strong motive for killing your husband, you can't prove you were where you say you were at the time of the murder, and the weapon used to kill him was found in a vehicle you own."

"What?"

This was clearly news to Theresa.

"The Audi Q7 was found in the car park of your tennis club in Les Martins. The knife that was used to kill

Arnold was in the glove compartment."

"Well I didn't put it there," Theresa said. "I told you I haven't driven that car in over a week."

"How do you think it ended up in your car?" O'Reilly said.

"I don't know."

"Right," O'Reilly said. "Let's say for argument's sake you didn't kill your husband. Can you think of anyone who would want to take his life? Did Arnold have any enemies?"

"Plenty. He was an arrogant bastard."

"And do you believe any of those enemies would want him dead?" O'Reilly said.

"No, of course not. This is unbelievable. I want to go home."

"That's not going to happen," O'Reilly told her. "We've got enough to charge you."

"What? You can't be serious?"

"I'm very serious."

"But I came here voluntarily. I was the one who came to you. I'm leaving right now."

"Theresa Green," O'Reilly said. "You're under arrest for the murder of Arnold Green."

He explained her rights and asked PC Hill to inform the duty sergeant.

CHAPTER SIXTEEN

When O'Reilly arrived at work the next morning there was a reception committee waiting for him outside the station. It consisted of only three people, but O'Reilly detested all of them. All of the main players from the Island Herald were standing outside the front gate.

Fred Viking spotted O'Reilly and soon a microphone was thrust in the Irishman's face.
"I believe you have the Green woman in custody," Fred said.

O'Reilly glared at him.

"Is it true?" Fred added. "Have you arrested Theresa Green for the murder of her husband?"

O'Reilly didn't reply.

"Come on, O'Reilly," Fred said. "You must have something to say. It's very rare for you to be lost for words."

O'Reilly did have some choice words for the editor of the Island Herald, but he decided not to voice them. Instead, he stepped closer to Fred Viking and mouthed two words that it wouldn't take an experienced lipreader to decipher. Feeling much better, he pushed past the three journalists and made his way inside the station.

"Mrs Green has demanded a lawyer," DC Stone told O'Reilly as soon as he stepped inside.

"I expected as much," O'Reilly said.

"What's the plan of action, sir? We're supposed to be bringing in her son this morning, aren't we?"

"We are," O'Reilly confirmed. "And it's important they don't speak to one another. Do you know who Mrs Green's lawyer is?"

"I can ask the duty sergeant. It'll be a bit tricky if it's the same one the kid has asked for."

"That won't happen, Andy. Can I have a quick word?"

"Of course, sir."

"In my office if you don't mind."

He nodded for DC Stone to go first and followed him down the corridor.

"Is something wrong, sir?" the shifty-eyed DC asked.

O'Reilly closed the door and told him to take a seat. "Assumpta told me you've asked her to move in with you," O'Reilly came straight out with it. "I was under the impression you still lived at home."

"I've been planning on moving out for a while. After my mum died, I really just stayed out of obligation to my dad, but he's doing much better now, and it's time I got a place of my own."

"And you want Assumpta to live with you?"

"I'm very fond of her, sir," DC Stone said. "I know you haven't always been happy about our relationship, but I really do like her. And I'll take good care of her."

"She's not a dog, man."

"I didn't mean..."

"Shut up," O'Reilly said. "I really can't understand what Assumpta sees in you, but it seems like there's nothing I can do about it. For what it's worth, you've got my blessing."

"Thank you, sir," DC Stone said.

He took a step forward and O'Reilly was worried he was going to embrace him. He took a step back.

"Don't, Andy," he warned. "Just don't."

"Sorry. I got a bit carried away there. Thank you. You won't regret it."

"And don't expect me to come apartment hunting with you," O'Reilly said. "You're on your own there. Right, now we've got that out of the way, you can leave me be for a moment. I need a cup of tea in my belly to figure out how best to proceed this morning."

* * *

James Green was dragged from a dream by an incessant banging noise. He'd been on a beach in Thailand. The Green family had taken a holiday there when James was thirteen. His sister was fifteen at the time, and her newfound interest in boys meant she rarely spent much time with the rest of the family.

James's parents were much closer back then and often they would embarrass the teenagers with their open displays of affection. Arnold and Theresa weren't shy when it came to kissing and cuddling in public.

James had dreamt about the beach he'd spent most of his time on. It was on the east side of a private island owned by a friend of the family. Situated on the southern tip of the Phi Phi Islands the island of Kho Phi Phi Lee was smack bang in the middle of the Andaman Sea and the beach was as close to paradise as James had ever been. The sea was a shade of blue he didn't know the name of, and it was as warm as bathwater. There was a natural break further out that meant the surf was never rough, and the sand on the beach was virgin white.

In the dream James was floating on his back a few metres from the shore. The only sound came from the gentle lapping of the waves on the beach. James had his eyes closed but he opened them when he heard the crack of a gunshot. When he turned his head, he saw a figure on the beach. The man was aiming the gun in his direction. James couldn't see the face of the gunman, but he seemed vaguely familiar.

Another shot rang out and James expected to feel the sting of the bullet as it passed through his body, but nothing happened. Another sound could be heard – a frantic splashing noise and when James located the source of it he realised that the man on the beach wasn't intent on shooting him after all.

The shark was about five metres away. At least one of the bullets had hit its target and the foam around the thrashing creature was stained pink. The third shot flew just inches past James's head, and the shark went still. As it sank down James took in the sight of it. One of the bullets had put a hole in its head and James determined this was the kill shot. As the shark sank deeper James looked into its eyes and started to shake. Here was a shark with a face that didn't belong there. The face James was staring at right now was his sister's face.

The banging carried on and James realised someone was knocking on his door. He rubbed his eyes and his gaze fell on the girl in the bed next to him. Sasha Hillman was clearly oblivious to the constant banging – she was sleeping the sleep of the dead next to him.

James got up and went to see who had woken him. He unlocked the door and stood face to face with Mr Graham. The old English teacher was standing outside with a grave expression on his face.
"What?" James said.
"The police are here," Mr Graham told him. "You have to go with them to St Peter Port."
"Can I at least get dressed first?"
"Of course," Mr Graham said. "I'll inform them you'll be along shortly."

Sasha Hillman coughed, and Mr Graham looked James in the eye.

"Is someone in here with you?"

James smiled and opened the door wider. Mr Graham looked inside, and his eyes grew wide behind his glasses.

"Sasha. What are you doing here?"

She stretched her arms and smiled too. "What do you think, Mr Graham?"

"This is outrageous," the English teacher said. "This is strictly against the rules. There will be serious consequences to this, you mark my words."

"What are you going to do, Mr Graham?" James said. "Inform Sasha's parents? Because the last time I checked she didn't have any."

CHAPTER SEVENTEEN

"Let's get started."

O'Reilly opted to have a briefing before doing anything else. James Green had been picked up and he was now waiting for his lawyer in a room not far from the room his mother had spent the night in. Neither of them were aware that the other was here, but O'Reilly knew it wouldn't be long before that changed. He wanted to run through the series of events once more before the Greens were interviewed.

"I want to discuss the murders of Arnold Green and John Hillman as connected crimes," he told the team. "I believe the same killer murdered them both. Does anyone disagree?"

"I still can't see how they can be connected."
It was DCI Fish. Even though he was the superior officer he'd never had a problem with O'Reilly heading up investigations. O'Reilly was far more experienced in the fine art of murder and DCI Fish was happy to let him lead.

"They're connected," O'Reilly insisted. "The two men lived next door to each other, and they were killed on the same day. We're looking at the same killer."

"What is Theresa Green's connection to John Hillman?" DC Stone wondered. "If we're assuming she was the one who killed her husband, why would she kill her neighbour too?"

"Perhaps he was a witness," DC Owen put forward. "Perhaps John Hillman saw what Theresa did and she killed him to keep him quiet."

"It's a plausible theory, Katie," O'Reilly said. "But a few things don't tie up with that theory. First, why wait so long to kill Mr Hillman? If Theresa suspected him of witnessing the murder of her husband, why wait so long to shut him up? The second thing that doesn't fit with the theory that John Hillman was killed to silence him is the fact that Theresa Green vanished for most of the day yesterday. She would be taking a huge risk in coming back so close to the scene of the murder of her husband. No, I think this is about something else altogether."

"What though?" DCI Fish said. "What is the connection between these two men besides the proximity of their homes?"

"I believe that will become clear in time," O'Reilly said. "I spoke to Mrs Green last night and she vehemently denies any involvement in the murder of her husband. She claims she was sailing alone, and she moored on Herm for the night."

"Can she corroborate it?" DS Skinner asked.

"She can't," O'Reilly said.

"Why didn't she answer her phone?" DC Owen said. "We tried calling her over ten times."

"She said the battery died."

"Very convenient," DC Stone said.

"It is. The dead battery not only explains why she wasn't aware that her husband was dead, but it also means her movements couldn't be traced via her mobile phone. Either she's telling the truth, or the dead battery is part of the plan."

"What else did she tell you?" DCI Fish said.

"Her husband was having an affair," O'Reilly said. "She said that's why she kicked him out."

"Did you ask her who the floozie is?" DC Stone said.

"There is such a thing as tact, Andy," DC Owen told him.

"No," O'Reilly said. "There is no such thing in a murder investigation. Andy's right – I ought to have got the name of the other woman. It'll be easy to check, but the fact that Arnold was having an affair is important."

"Another motive then," DC Owen decided.

"They just keep stacking up," O'Reilly said. "We know she stands to inherit a big fat zero in the event of a divorce, but she gets close to thirty million with him dead. She gets the cash, and she gets one up on the bit on the side into the bargain, but I'm still smelling a rat. Does anyone else think something smells a bit off here?"

The room was silent.

"Where does John Hillman come into the equation?" DC Owen was the first to speak.

"Where indeed?" O'Reilly said. "And I'm afraid I don't have the answer to that question. Let's look at what we have. Arnold Green was killed between two and three yesterday morning. The knife that was used to kill him was discovered in his wife's car, and she claims she hasn't driven the vehicle for over a week. John Hillman was killed later that day. The missing 9 iron golf club is probably what was used to attack him, and that has yet to be recovered. Does anyone have any suggestions as to what this could be about?"

"Do we know if John Hillman had money?" DC Stone asked.

"His address suggests he does," O'Reilly said. "The houses in that part of Vazon are extremely expensive, as is the school Mr Hillman's daughter attends. We don't know the details of his fortune, but we can find out. Mr Hillman's wife died when Sasha was eleven. Cancer, and he's brought her up on his own."

"So there's nobody who stands to inherit his money besides the daughter?" DC Owen said.

"That too will become clear during the course of the day. But I'm not sure this is as simple as a murder for money – there's more to it than that. I can feel it."

PC London entered the room.

"Sorry to interrupt, but James Green's lawyer has arrived."

"Thanks, Kim," O'Reilly said. "We'll get to him as soon as we've finished."

"Greg told me something interesting, sir," PC London said. "When they went to pick the boy up, the English teacher had something to tell them."

"Go on."

"Greg said the teacher went to fetch James and he found a fellow student in the room with him."

"That's nothing to concern us."

"I think it might be, sir," PC London said. "It was a girl – she'd obviously been there all night with James, and it was Sasha Hillman. James spent the night with the daughter of the second victim."

CHAPTER EIGHTEEN

O'Reilly was planning on speaking to Theresa Green again but after what PC London had told him he decided to leave that up to DCI Fish and DS Skinner. He wanted to know what was going on between James and Sasha Hillman. It was extremely suspicious that she'd fled the scene of her father's murder and made her way straight to the room of the son of the first victim, and O'Reilly wanted an explanation.

James's lawyer was a weedy little man with a thin moustache. His eyes were emotionless behind the John Lennon glasses. He'd introduced himself as Jarrod Henshaw and O'Reilly deduced he worked for the same firm as Stephan Brown. DC Owen did the honours with the recording device and O'Reilly got the ball rolling.

"James," he said. "How are you feeling?"

"My client is not here to discuss his emotional state." Jarrod Henshaw fixed O'Reilly with an icy stare when he said this.

"Grand," O'Reilly said. "James, we'd like to ask you a few more questions. Can you explain why Sasha Hillman was in your room at the school this morning?"

"My client is sixteen," Jarrod said. "As is Sasha. What happens between them is not your concern."

"I'll be the judge of that. James, could you please answer the question."

"What's the big deal?" the teenage boy asked. "We're not kids."

"Was Sasha with you the whole night?" DC Owen said.

"What of it? We like each other. She's just found her dad dead, and I'd say that bonds us together, wouldn't you?"

"What do you mean by that?" O'Reilly said.

"Both of us have lost our fathers. Both of us were the ones to find their bodies. What do you think I meant by it?"

"That's quite a coincidence," DC Owen commented.

"I don't like what you're implying, young lady," Jarrod Henshaw interrupted.

"Detective Owen isn't implying anything," O'Reilly said. "She is merely stating a fact. James, how long have you and Sasha been in a relationship?"

"We're not in a relationship," James said.

"And yet you spent the night together."

"This is the twenty-first century, granddad. Shit happens."

O'Reilly was starting to really dislike this sixteen-year-old boy.

"Did Sasha tell you what happened to her father?" he said.

"Of course," James said. "That's why she came to me. She was in shock, and she needed someone to talk to."

"And you didn't think to inform anyone she was with you?" DC Owen said. "You must have known we'd be looking for her after she disappeared from the house next door."

"It's a free country," James said and turned to his lawyer. "That's right, isn't it?"

"That's right," Jarrod confirmed. "Neither Sasha nor my client has broken any laws, and I would suggest you either get to the point or you allow James to go home."

"There's the problem right there," O'Reilly said. "We can't do that. James's father is dead, and his mother is in custody."

This was clearly news to James Green. "What?"

"Your mother was arrested for the murder of your dad last night," DC Owen explained. "She will no doubt be charged during the course of the day."

"Therein lies the problem you see," O'Reilly said. "You're only sixteen, James. In the eyes of the law, you are not yet old enough to be left to your own devices."

A smile formed on James Green's face and O'Reilly felt something stir in the pit of his stomach. It wasn't a pleasant sensation, and he knew it didn't bode well. Jarrod Henshaw opened up a file and retrieved a single piece of paper. He perused it for a moment and passed it across the table to O'Reilly.

"What's this?" the Irishman asked.

"Read it," Jarrod said. "This is a document that ought to clarify a few things for you."

O'Reilly started to read. A lot of the language was complicated but once he'd got through the longwinded legalese the gist of the document became clear. He handed the paper to DC Owen to read.

"This is a section of Arnold Green's Last Will and Testament that pertains to the wellbeing of the children in the event of Mr Green's demise occurring before they reach the age of eighteen," Jarrod Henshaw explained. "As you can see there's a Testamentary Guardianship clause. Section 5 of the Children's Act of 1989 is included on the back for reference purposes. According to the act, in the event of the death of one or both parents a testamentary guardian can be appointed. There is a grandmother in Australia who is named, but as you can understand that's hardly practical, and an additional clause was added to the guardianship section. There is another name in there, and the person named is in a position to legally take care of James. It's Vanessa Green who is named in the Will."

"This is nonsense," O'Reilly scoffed.

"It's the law, Detective."

"But Mrs Green is very much alive," DC Owen pointed out. "This says that Vanessa will only become James's legal guardian on the event of both parents dying. James's mother isn't dead."

"Why did you even bring this today?" O'Reilly asked.

"DC Owen is right – Theresa Green is alive."

"And, as you've already stated," Jarrod said. "She's

been arrested for the murder of Arnold, and she will be charged with that crime in due course. If she's convicted, she will receive the mandatory life sentence as set out by law. She will be unable to care for my client and as such the Testamentary Guardianship clause will come into effect."

"I think we can conclude there," O'Reilly decided.

"I agree," Jarrod said. "I don't believe there's anything more to discuss, is there?"

"Interview with James Green ended, 11:22," O'Reilly said and stopped the tape.

"I presume my client is free to go."

"For now," O'Reilly said. "But don't leave town, James. I've got a feeling we'll be chatting again very soon."

CHAPTER NINETEEN

"This case has taken a very different turn, hasn't it?" O'Reilly was sitting in his office with DC Owen. DCI Fish had outlined the outcome of the second interview with Theresa Green and she'd stuck to her story. She'd spent the night on her yacht in Herm and she was nowhere near Guernsey when her husband was killed. She still couldn't provide them with corroboration of this and in all likelihood, she would be charged with Arnold Green's murder. The knife in her car, the motive in the form of Arnold's Will and the lack of an alibi would be enough for the CPS to come to that decision. But it didn't sit well with O'Reilly.

"I don't think she did it, Katie," he said. He sipped his tea and sighed.

"What about the knife in her car?" DC Owen said. "She can't account for her movements at the time of

Arnold's murder, and she has a very strong motive."
"Doesn't it all feel a bit convenient? She has no alibi - she stands to inherit millions, and the weapon that was used to kill her husband was in a rather obvious place. Either she's a really inept murderer or she didn't kill him. She would know she would be the first person we would look into. Thirty million is a real incentive to end someone's life. Why would she leave the knife in a car in a place where she's known to frequent? This is the most obvious set up I've ever come across."
"Who would do that?" DC Owen asked. "Who would want to set her up for the murder of her husband?"
"It's starting to look like James Green is deeply involved in this."
"He's sixteen years old, sir," DC Owen said. "He's a schoolboy."
"And he's a cool customer. You saw how he acted in the interview. Most kids his age would be shitting in their pants under those circumstances, but James acted like he was in total control. And I'm getting the feeling that's because he is in control. He's calling the shots, but I don't know what he's planning."

The sound of his ringtone cut short the conversation. O'Reilly saw from the screen that it was

Victoria Radcliffe. He debated whether to answer it, but he let it ring out. He would call his fiancé back when he'd finished discussing the confusion around the recent murders.

"James stands to inherit five million," DC Owen said. "When he's eighteen he'll be incredibly rich. But that's in two years' time. If he is involved in the death of his father, why do it now? Why not wait until he can get hold of the money?"

"Perhaps that's precisely why he chose to do it now," O'Reilly suggested.

"If his father was killed right after James reached the age of eighteen, it would seem suspicious."

"Exactly. We need to locate his sister. If what that lawyer said is true and Vanessa has been named as James's legal guardian, where is she? Why hasn't she been informed? The world is a much smaller place than it used to be, and it isn't hard to find someone if you look hard enough. Why hasn't that law firm made any effort to contact the sister?"

"Do you think she could also be involved?" DC Owen said.

"How? She's travelling around southeast Asia. And I don't know many eighteen-year-old girls who would relish the thought of having to look after a little brother."

"I suppose that's true. What do we do now?"

"Theresa Green will be charged with her husband's murder," O'Reilly said. "Of that I'm sure, so we look more closely at John Hillman."

"Do you still believe they're connected?"

"Without a doubt. We'll discuss Mr Hillman in the afternoon briefing. Go and get yourself some lunch. I'm going to find a bench by the beach to sit on while I phone my fiancé back."

"Have you set a date yet?"

"I have no idea, Katie," O'Reilly said. "I don't think I'm involved in that part of things. Summi and Victoria won't thank me if I stick my nose in."

"How is Assumpta?"

"Mad in the fekkin head. She's talking about moving in with Andy."

"I think they make a great couple."

"Then there's something also not right with your head," O'Reilly told her. "Get yourself off for an hour. Briefing at one."

The walk down to the promenade didn't seem like such a good idea when O'Reilly got to his feet and his leg complained so much he had to sit right back down again. He stretched out and managed to ease the pain a little. He couldn't understand what was wrong – he'd followed the doctor's advice, and he'd done all the exercises suggested by the physiotherapist, but the bone was still giving him problems. He wondered if he ought to make an appointment to see the doctor but he decided not to. He would give it some more time – that's all he needed. Time healed all wounds.

He made another cup of tea and dialled Victoria's number. She answered just as O'Reilly was about to hang up and the tone of her voice told him she was out of breath.

"Liam," she gasped.

"Is everything alight?" O'Reilly asked.

He heard her take a few deep breaths. Then she laughed.

"Sorry. I forgot where I'd put my phone, and it also took me a while to register it actually was my ringtone I was hearing. I was running around like a headless chicken to try and find it. It's the radiation treatment – it makes my head a bit foggy. How are you?"

"Grand."

He wasn't going to burden her with the pain in his leg. A broken femur paled into insignificance compared with what she was dealing with.

"I missed your call," he added.

"I know you're busy," Victoria said. "But I was wondering what you were up to later."

"Babysitting of a couple of freeloading moggies," he said. "Same old, same old. What did you have in mind?"

"A bite to eat and a bit of wedding talk."

"I like the sound of the first part."

"I want you to be involved, Liam," Victoria said.

"And I will be involved," O'Reilly promised. "I'll even buy a new suit."

"We'll discuss it later. How does the Red Snapper sound?"

"It sounds great to me. Are you sure you don't want to go somewhere closer to your side of the island?"

"You make it sound like we're a thousand miles from each other. Red Snapper it is then. Eight sharp."

"It's a date," O'Reilly said. "Are you at the shop?"

"I had a bit of a funny turn earlier, and Tommy ordered me to take the afternoon off."

"You've gotta love big brothers," O'Reilly said. "What was this funny turn?"

"Nothing serious. I just felt a bit faint for a while. It soon passed."

"Glad to hear it," O'Reilly said. "See you at eight."

He ended the call and finished his tea. The ache in his leg still lingered but there was a much stronger twinge niggling at his insides than that. It was a sense that something in the investigation was all wrong. There was much more to these murders than what lay on the surface and as much as O'Reilly tried to scrape away the scum on the top, he couldn't quite see what was hidden beneath.

A third pang was also making its presence known. His stomach was telling him he hadn't eaten anything today. The five cups of tea just wouldn't cut it – he needed something substantial in his belly, and he needed it now.

CHAPTER TWENTY

After a stodgy lunch that now sat heavy in his stomach, O'Reilly began the afternoon briefing. He wanted to discuss the murder of John Hillman in more detail. The forensic team hadn't finished with the house and there wasn't much to go on from that perspective, but O'Reilly wanted to talk about John Hillman the man. Why did someone attack him in his own home with one of his golf clubs? DC Stone and DS Skinner had spoken to a few of John's friends the previous day and O'Reilly hoped they would have something to kickstart the investigation into his death.

He didn't get the chance. DI Peters came inside the room, and he'd come bearing gifts. The laptop he was carrying told O'Reilly he had something to tell them.

"Jim," he said. "What have you got for us? Have you finished at John Hillman's house?"

"Henry and Glenda are still there," DI Peters said. "I've got some news on the first one. I can tell you there is nothing yet to link the boy to the murder of his father. His prints weren't on the knife, nor were there any of his prints inside the Audi."

"Isn't that strange?" DC Owen said. "Surely some of his fingerprints would be in his mother's car."

"I'm just telling you what I found. It's up to you what to make of that information."

"What have you got to tell us?" O'Reilly asked.

DI Peters flipped open his laptop and booted it up. It didn't take long. He tapped the keypad, and an image appeared on the screen.

"The hidden compartment behind the bookcase was really bugging me," he said. "I knew there was something behind those shelves and I wasn't mistaken."

"You managed to open it?" O'Reilly said.

"It came to me in the middle of the night," DI Peters explained. "As most sudden insights are wont to do."

"What?" It was DC Stone.

"You'll understand when you get your first inspirational insight, Andy," O'Reilly informed him.

"I recalled the books that weren't actual books," DI Peters continued. "A random selection ranging from Crime to Classics, and I also remembered something about the positioning of them. There was no real order. A Virginia Woolf was next to a collection of Ian Rankin. The early Rebus books. Classics. Then there was a couple of Stephen King horrors."

"How did you open it?" O'Reilly said.

"I pressed my fingers on three of the book spines at the same time. And the panel slid open."

"But how did you know which books to press?" DC Stone wondered.

"They were the only ones with green spines."

"Arnold Green," O'Reilly said. "Simple but effective. Did you find much behind the bookcase?"

"I did. This is what it looks like behind there."

The team gathered around to look at the screen. The space behind the bookcase wasn't simply a hidden compartment - it was a proper room.

"Holy cow," DC Stone exclaimed.

"Eloquently put, Andy," O'Reilly said. "But it is rather extraordinary."

"I've never seen anything like it," DS Skinner said. "Why would someone have a secret room in their house?"

"I believe it's some kind of panic room," DI Peters told him. "I found a control panel at the side of the room. There are numerous screens and I think they're linked up to cameras somewhere in the house. The system is password protected so we're going to need to get some experts to look at it."

He tapped the keypad again and another image appeared on the screen.

"There is a refrigerator," DI Peters said. "And a store cupboard, fully stocked with food. I'd estimate there to be enough food and water to last at least a month. There's even a small bathroom cubicle on the other side. This is a seriously well-thought-out room."

"Did you find anything to indicate that anyone had been in there recently?" O'Reilly asked.

"There was nothing to suggest it in the form of clothing, cups and plates and the like," DI Peters said. "But there was a smell."

"A smell?" DC Stone repeated.

"A sweet floral smell. I think it was perfume and if I'm not mistaken I'd say it was Anais Anais."

"Anais what?" DC Stone said.

"It's a perfume made by Cacharel," DC Owen educated him.

"That's correct," DI Peters said. "My wife sometimes wears it. I believe a woman was in the panic room recently and her perfume lingered. But that's not all I found."

Another tap of the keypad and an image of something familiar filled the screen.

"I found this in the food cupboard behind some boxes of cereal," DI Peters said.

"It's a golf club," DC Stone stated the obvious.

"A number nine club to be more precise," DI Peters said. "A club from a Calloway set. They're very exclusive golf clubs, and they can only be purchased in Scotland. John Powell just happened to have a set of these, and the nine iron was missing."

The room fell silent for a moment. Everyone in the team were processing what this new information meant.

"How?" O'Reilly was the first to ask the question on everyone's lips. "How on earth did the weapon that was used to kill a man end up in a panic room next door?"

"And why did it end up there?" DC Owen asked. "Why did it end up in the secret room of a man who had been brutally murdered only hours earlier?"

CHAPTER TWENTY ONE

"This just gets more and more complicated by the second."

O'Reilly was trying to make sense of what DI Peters had discovered.

"How did they even get into the secret room?" he added. "The street has been swarming with police since Arnold Green's body was found. Why didn't anyone see anything?"

"We might get something from the CCTV cameras," DC Stone said. "The ones linked to the control panel in the panic room."

"DI Peters has informed the IT team," O'Reilly told him. "I don't think it'll take them long to retrieve whatever footage is on there. I don't mind admitting that this one has got me well and truly stumped."

"Where does Theresa Green fit into this?" DC Owen said. "We don't know where she was at the time John Hillman was murdered, and she will have known about the secret room behind the bookcase."

"But it still doesn't explain how she managed to get inside the house without being seen," DS Skinner joined in.

"Was the house sealed off the whole time?" DCI Fish asked. "Did we have officers there all night?"

It took one phone call to find out if this was the case, and the answer DC Owen got when she asked PC Kim London wasn't the one O'Reilly had hoped for. "This is unbelievable," he said. "That house should have been sealed off."

According to PC London there had been nobody stationed on La Rue Mere between two and eight that morning. O'Reilly cursed himself. He should have made sure someone was keeping an eye on the house twenty-four-seven, and he knew he'd made a huge blunder. He told the team as much.

"Don't beat yourself up about it," DCI Fish said. "You weren't to know there would be another murder right next door."

"It doesn't matter," O'Reilly argued. "I should have insisted that the house stayed off limits. I messed up."

"Hindsight is a wonderful thing, Liam," DCI Fish added. "What's done is done. We need to move forward."

"With what? What exactly do we have to work with? A woman is going to be charged with a murder she did not commit, and the real killer is still out there somewhere. We have a golf club that was used to kill another man, but we haven't a fekkin clue how it ended up in a secret room next door. I don't know what's going on here, Tom."

"What do we know about John Hillman?" DCI Fish changed the subject rather obviously.

"Andy and I spoke to a few of his friends," DS Skinner said. "John was a decent man according to all of them. He was a diligent worker and a devoted father. He's been a single parent since his wife succumbed to cancer five years ago, and by all accounts he's done a great job."

"Nobody had a bad word to say about him," DC Stone said.

"They never do, do they?" O'Reilly said. "People are reluctant to speak ill of the dead."

"I got the impression they were being genuine, sir," DS Skinner said. "John was an-all round good guy."

"What did he do for a living?" DCI Fish asked.

"Something in IT," DC Stone replied rather vaguely.

"It must have been something important," O'Reilly said. "I don't know what the house prices in Rue La Mere are like, but I can imagine they're pretty pricey, and the school Sasha attends isn't cheap either."

"The average price for a property in Rue La Mere is in the region of ten million," DC Owen said. "I checked. And the school fees for Vazon High start at around fifty thousand a year. More if you're a boarder."

"That's more than any of us earn in a year," DC Stone pointed out.

"John Hillman was a considerably wealthy man," O'Reilly said.

"And according to the people we spoke to," DS Skinner said. "Sasha is an only child, so it's safe to assume she'll inherit that money now."

"There's something going on with Sasha and James Green," O'Reilly said.

"Are you suggesting she was involved in her father's murder?" DC Stone said.

"It needs to be considered."

"But she was at school when John was murdered, wasn't she?"

"We haven't yet confirmed that, Andy. Dr Lille has put his time of death between noon and three yesterday."

"Then Sasha must have been at school," DCI Fish decided.

"Katie," O'Reilly said. "Could you find out please. Check her timetable for yesterday and also check that she was in the classes she was supposed to be in."

"Will do, sir," DC Owen said and left the briefing room.

"Is Theresa Green out of the running for John Hillman's murder?" DC Stone asked.

"As far as I'm concerned, she is," O'Reilly confirmed. "I don't believe she killed her husband, and she had no reason to want her neighbour dead."

"So that leaves the kids then," DS Skinner reckoned.

"Two sixteen-year-old schoolkids," O'Reilly said. "Both set to become extremely wealthy. So far, forensics have found nothing that links James Green to the murder of his father. No evidence suggesting he was anywhere near Arnold Green recently. No hairs or fibres, and no fingerprints on the murder weapon."

"It's possible he disposed of the clothes he was wearing after he carried out the murder," DS Skinner put forward. "And he could have wiped the knife clean when he hid it in his mother's car."

"That ties in with why there were none of James's prints in the Audi," DC Stone said. "He could have wiped the whole vehicle clean. I still think it's iffy that his prints weren't anywhere inside that vehicle. He will have travelled in it loads of times."

"Are we all on the same page then?" O'Reilly asked. "Are we all of the opinion that James Green and Sasha Hillman are our priority right now?"
The nods around the table told him they were united in the belief that the most probable suspects in a double murder investigation were two students from Vazon High School.

CHAPTER TWENTY TWO

"I'm in."

Derek Nunn had only just moved to the island from Newcastle. He'd recently divorced and the advert for the IT position within the Island Police had grabbed him from the moment he laid eyes on it. He needed a new start and where better to start again than on an island miles away from anywhere. Derek hadn't expected life to flow at such a slow pace, and the call from DI Peters had been the first promise of a bit of excitement since accepting the IT job with the Island Police.

"I won't ask how you did it," DI Peters said. The Head of Forensics wasn't very clued up where IT was concerned.

"People think passwords are the ultimate protection," Derek told him, nevertheless. "They're not. I used a rainbow table. It figures out every possible password up to fourteen characters then stores them in a database. It allows me to compare the encrypted values and it will get me in in no time at all. My record is fifteen seconds."

DI Peters had no idea what he was talking about, and his thick Geordie accent didn't help matters.

"Can you access the CCTV footage?" he said.

"Already onto it," Derek said. "That is, I would be if there was any footage to access."

"What do you mean?"

"You're looking for the footage from yesterday?"

"That's right," DI Peters said. "Between ten and three in the afternoon."

Derek's fingers flew across the keyboard on his laptop.

"There's nowt here."

"Are you sure?" DI Peters said.

"The cameras were active yesterday," Derek told him. "Early on, that is. There's four of them – in the kitchen, living room, entrance hall and sitting room, but there's nothing there after seven yesterday morning."

"What does that mean?"

"There's only two explanations," Derek said. "Either the cameras were switched off or they were on, and someone deleted the footage."

DI Peters didn't know what to do. It was pretty obvious that whoever put the golf club in the secret room knew about the cameras, and it was also clear that they knew how to disarm them.

"OK," he said. "What's on the footage from earlier?"

Derek tapped his keypad and rewound the footage to one minute past midnight on the day of the murders. He then sped it up to ten times speed.

"There's nowt here," he said after a few minutes had passed. "Absolutely sod all. Perhaps everyone was asleep."

"Keep watching," DI Peters said. "Whoever deleted those files had to walk past at least one of those cameras to get into the secret room. They will have been caught in the action."

"Not necessarily."

DI Peters looked at him. "I'm not following you."

"This is a fancy system," Derek said. "Must have cost a few bob, and it'll probably all be linked to the operator's mobile phone. It's pretty common with most systems. People like to see what's going on when they're not at home. And I'm pretty sure this system can be controlled remotely too."

"On a mobile phone?"

Derek nodded. "Those cameras could have been disabled from anywhere on the island. Same goes for the footage. Anyone with admin access would be able to delete any footage they didn't want."

* * *

"We have a problem."

They were the four words that O'Reilly detested more than any other, and when they were spoken by someone like DC Owen, he knew she wasn't playing around.

O'Reilly sighed. "What is it, Katie?"

"Sasha Hillman has an alibi for the time her father was murdered, sir."

"Is it reliable?"

"That's the problem," DC Owen said. "Her alibi is James Green."

"Then it's not reliable."

"That's not the only problem. Sasha claims she spoke to one of the teachers before she went to talk to James. The teacher confirmed it. Sasha was at school all day yesterday, and James Green never left the school grounds either."

"He refused to leave, didn't he?" O'Reilly remembered.

"That's right. After his episode in class, he refused to go, and the Head of School offered him a room."

"Damn it, Katie," O'Reilly said. "What the hell is going on here?"

"I thought the Irish frowned upon biblical curses, sir," DC Owen said. "You've just used two in one sentence."

"It's acceptable at times like these. If it wasn't those kids, who else do we look at?"

"It's possible they're still involved, sir," DC Owen said. "Just because they didn't carry out the actual murders, it doesn't put them in the clear."

"No, it doesn't. I want to speak to the Super about hauling them both in and keeping them here."

"Are we going to arrest them?"

"If I can persuade the Super, we are," O'Reilly said. "I want access to their phones and their other mobile devices. I want to look through every message they've ever sent and every call they've ever made, but to do that I need a damn good reason to do so. And before you chastise me for cursing, that wasn't a proper one. Those kids are involved in this, and I want to know what that involvement is."

CHAPTER TWENTY THREE

"Mrs Dodds, if you could just sign here, here and here."

Jane Dodds slipped her reading glasses down and perused the document on the table.

"It's a standard deed of sale."

Jane picked up the pen and put her signature where she'd been instructed to.

"Now, if you could just initial each page, we'll get the ball rolling. As you must appreciate, this is a very generous price. Especially in light of the shenanigans on the street recently."

Jane thought this was a peculiar way to put it. In her opinion two brutal murders hardly constituted *shenanigans*, but the lawyer was right – it was a really good deal. Jane had been meaning to sell anyway, and now she and Benjamin would be able to buy something smaller and more manageable. The children were long gone and the huge house on Rue La Mere was a bit excessive now there was just Benjamin and Jane.

"All done."

The lawyer grinned a shark's smile and collected up the documents.

"A copy will be emailed to you in due course, and once the documents are processed at the Deeds Office the funds will be transferred to your account. The firm will expedite the process, you'll be pleased to hear."
"How long are we talking about?" Jane asked.
"It shouldn't take longer than a couple of weeks. We've got ways of speeding up the process."
The lawyer tapped his nose and Jane had a sudden urge to tell him to get the hell out of her house while it was still her house.

She didn't.
"Is that it then?" she asked instead.
"That's it," the lawyer confirmed. "There's nothing more you need to concern yourself with. Although you might want to think about making a start on packing up your things. I can give you the details of some reliable removal companies if you like."
"That won't be necessary," Jane said. "I can't wait to tell my husband the good news."
"Good news indeed."
Something in the way the lawyer spoke the words gave Jane a funny feeling in her stomach. She didn't know what it was, but she didn't like it one little bit.

"Benjamin is still having doubts," she said.

"That's only natural. This property has been a big part of your lives for a very long time, but once the deal is done, you'll be able to begin a new chapter in your lives."

"I understand there is a cooling-off period?" Jane said. "In case we have a change of heart."

"Of course. It is your right to do just that, but I don't think that's going to be a problem for us." He paused for a moment and added: "is it?"

"Probably not," Jane said.

"I'll see myself out."

Jane watched as the lawyer got to his feet and left her alone. She heard the front door slam and everything was quiet.

* * *

"It's your decision, Liam."

Superintendent Hayes sounded irritated, and O'Reilly wondered if he'd caught her at a bad time.

"I just needed someone to tell me it's the right one," he said. "Arresting a couple of teenagers is risky."

"Do we have grounds to justify it?"

"I think we do. Both of them stand to gain considerably from the deaths of their fathers and their alibis are very suspect. Sasha is claiming that James was with her at the time of John Hillman's murder, and I find that very convenient. We interviewed the boy earlier and he was far too cool under the circumstances. In my experience that stinks of the arrogance of someone who thinks they've got away with something. They're involved in this, Ma'am."

"Then do what you have to do."

"Is everything alright?" O'Reilly asked.

"Everything's fine," Superintendent Hayes replied. O'Reilly didn't believe her, but he didn't press the matter.

"Grand," he said. "I'm sure Tom will keep you up to date."

"I imagine he will," Superintendent Hayes said. There was a pause in the conversation and when O'Reilly filled the silence the monotonous tone on the other end of the line told him he was talking to himself. Superintendent Hayes had hung up.

O'Reilly leaned back in his chair and exhaled a long breath of air. He needed a moment to gather his thoughts, and right now those thoughts were rather blurred. Two men had been murdered, and the two people suspected of being involved in their deaths were squeaky clean as far as the evidence was concerned. A woman was in custody because all of the evidence pointed in her direction, but O'Reilly was convinced she wasn't involved. It truly was the most bizarre series of events he'd ever encountered, and he didn't know how to move past the confusion. Usually, in a murder investigation there was something in the details that gave him a break, but in this instance, he couldn't see anything. He had two neighbours. The men were killed within hours of each other, and in both instances the weapons used to kill them had been found. The knife in Theresa Green's car had sounded some obvious alarm bells but the golf club in the panic room of the house next door was baffling.

O'Reilly's phone started to ring, and he found himself staring at the screen and wondering whether to answer it. He was getting tired of it. The small, innocuous device had been the bearer of bad news for far too long. This time was no different.

"Sir."

It was PC London.

"What is it, Kim?" O'Reilly asked her.

"We've got another dead man, sir."

"Go on," O'Reilly urged.

"Benjamin Dodds," PC London said. "He injured himself playing bowls..."

"You're calling about a bowls-related death?" O'Reilly interrupted.

"Of course not. Mr Dodds called his wife to tell her what had happened, and said he was coming home early. He didn't arrive back, so his wife called the bowls club, and the manager said he'd been there that afternoon, but he thought he'd left. He found him on the floor of the changing room. It looks like he's been beaten to death."

"Benjamin Dodds," O'Reilly said. "Why does that name ring a bell?"

"Because you've spoken to him, sir," PC London said. "He lives at number 6 Rue La Mere."

CHAPTER TWENTY FOUR

O'Reilly had a lot on his mind. There had been times since his arrival on the island that he'd found himself with very little to do. The crime on the small piece of rock called Guernsey was nothing compared to the hustle and bustle of his hometown. In Dublin there had always been something to occupy his time, and he'd grown used to it. He'd also grown accustomed to the quiet times in Guernsey but now he found himself with far too much to think about. His to-do list was getting longer and longer every minute, and O'Reilly wasn't sure how to cope with it.

In the end he decided to delegate. He sent DS Skinner and DC Stone to the Vazon Bowls Club to speak to the people Benjamin Dodds was playing with that afternoon. He knew that DI Peters would already be there, and that put his mind at ease somewhat. According to PC London, Benjamin had been beaten to death in the changing room of the club. It was very risky doing that during the day and O'Reilly knew the murder would have to have been carried out quickly. There was hope there. It was highly likely the killer would have left something behind, and if that was the case DI Peters would find it.

They still needed to bring James Green and Sasha Hillman in for questioning, but O'Reilly decided to push that further down the list. He knew beyond a shadow of a doubt that there was something that connected the three dead men and for that reason he took yet another trip to Rue La Mere. The exclusive street in Vazon had suddenly become the murder capital of the island.

"Mrs Dodds is home," O'Reilly told DC Owen. "PC Hill told me her sister came over as soon as she heard the news. The sister seems to know the score, and she's expecting us."

DC Owen parked her car outside number 6 and switched off the engine.

"We've never come across anything like this, have we?" she said.

"I don't think anyone has, Katie," O'Reilly said. "Three dead men, all from the same street. It's like something from a far-fetched Hollywood movie."

He rang the bell and the door to number 6 was opened by a woman who looked to be in her sixties. She was tall and slim, and her grey hair was long. O'Reilly told her who they were, and the woman introduced herself as Brenda Coleman. She was Jane Dodds's sister.

"How is she?" O'Reilly asked.

"Bearing up," Brenda said. "I don't think it's quite sunk in yet. I suppose you ought to come in."

She told them that Jane was in the conservatory at the back of the house, and she led the way. She offered them something to drink but O'Reilly declined. He'd overdosed on tea today and he didn't think he could stomach another cup. He took a seat opposite Jane Dodds.

"Mrs Dodds," he began. "We're very sorry about Benjamin."

Jane nodded and rubbed her eyes. "I didn't believe it when George told me."

"George is the manager of the bowls club," Brenda explained.

"Who would do such a thing?" Jane asked. "Benjamin wouldn't hurt a fly."

"We're going to find out," O'Reilly promised. "Are you up to answering a few questions?"

Jane nodded again.

A mobile phone ringtone sounded somewhere close by but nobody made any effort to go and answer it.

"The press have already found out what happened," Brenda said. "There have been over a dozen calls already."

"They're a real nuisance," O'Reilly said.

"How did they find out so quickly?"

"They have their ways."

The phone stopped ringing and started again.

"I'll go and switch it off," Brenda said.

She left the room and didn't return.

"Can you think of anyone who would want to hurt your husband?" O'Reilly asked Jane.

"Of course not," she said. "He was a wonderful man."

"Who knew that Benjamin would be playing bowls today?" DC Owen said.

"He plays every Friday. Has done for years."

"And this was common knowledge?" O'Reilly said.

"What are you saying?" Jane said.

"We're just trying to get a picture of what happened. It's possible that whoever attacked your husband knew his routine."

"Are you suggesting this was someone we know?"

"It usually is," DC Owen told her. "The majority of murders are carried out by people known to the victim."

For the first time since they'd arrived cracks began to appear in Jane Dodds's cool veneer. Her bottom lip started to quiver, and she wiped a tear from her eye. "I'm sorry. It just doesn't seem real. Sitting here listening to you talk about *murders* and *victims* feels rather surreal. This is something that happens to other people, isn't it?"

"We'll try not to keep you much longer," O'Reilly said. "Can you tell us a bit about what Benjamin was like? How long have you been married?"

"Thirty-two years," Jane replied.

"Do you have any children?" DC Owen asked.

"Two. A girl and a boy. They've left the island now. That's one of the reasons why I'm selling my house."

"The house is on the market?" O'Reilly said.

"Not exactly," Jane said. "It's already been sold. The lawyer came round with the papers for me to sign earlier."

"Why are you selling?" DC Owen said.

"This place is far too big for the two of us," Jane said. "It was great when the children were still living here, but now it's just Benjamin and I, it seemed silly to keep it."

"I suppose it is rather too much for two people," O'Reilly agreed.

"And now it's just me," Jane said and sniffed loudly.

"It's alright, Mrs Dodds," DC Owen said.

She found a box of tissues on the coffee table and handed Jane a couple.

"Is this going to take much longer?" Jane said and blew her nose. "I really need to inform Fiona and Frank what's happened."

"Fiona and Frank are your children?" DC Owen said.

"They need to know. I don't want them finding out by reading the papers."

"Of course," O'Reilly said. "Just a couple more questions. Did you know your neighbours very well? The Greens and the Hillmans?"

"As well as anyone knows their neighbours these days," Jane said. "Why do you ask?"

"Arnold Green and John Hillman were murdered recently," O'Reilly said. "And we need to find out if there's a connection between Benjamin and them."

"Well I can tell you there isn't. Besides them being neighbours."

"Do you socialise with your neighbours?" DC Owen asked.

"Hardly ever," Jane said. "Harold and Theresa have only lived on the street for a few years, and we've barely spoken in that time."

"What about the Hillmans?" O'Reilly said. "How long have they been on Rue La Mere?"

"About fifteen years," Jane said. "I think they moved here when Sasha was a baby."

"Do you know Sasha Hillman then?" O'Reilly said.

"Only to say hello to. She seems like a nice girl."

"Do you know James Green too?"

"Him, I don't like," Jane said.

"Why don't you like him?"

"I don't know. There's something not quite right about him. It's not something I can really explain, but I sense something *off* in him."

O'Reilly got to his feet.

"I think that's enough questions for now. We might need to talk to you again."

DC Owen stood up too.

"We're very sorry for your loss, Mrs Dodds."

More tears appeared in Jane's eyes. She wiped them away and looked at O'Reilly.

"What exactly happened to him? I was only told that Benjamin was attacked, and he didn't survive. Do you think he suffered?"

O'Reilly didn't know the details of the attack.

"It was very quick," he said anyway. "It was all over in a flash."

CHAPTER TWENTY FIVE

"I can't see the point of bowls."

DC Stone looked over at the bowling green. The lawn was immaculate. There wasn't a brown patch in sight. It was clear that whoever was in charge of maintaining the green kept on top of things.

"Old man's marbles," DS Skinner said. "That's what my dad used to call it. Old man's marbles. He always said he wouldn't be seen dead playing bowls, and now he plays twice a week. He reckons it's great exercise and it's a good way to socialise."

"It didn't do Benjamin Dodds any favours, did it?" DC Stone pointed out.

A tall man dressed in bowls whites approached. He was very tanned, and he looked to be in his fifties.

"Are you from the police?" he asked DC Stone.

"That's right," the rat-eyed DC said. "I'm DC Stone and this is DS Skinner."

"Is there somewhere we can talk in private?" DS Skinner said.

He nodded to the group of men and women standing to the side of the green. A few of them were taking a keen interest in the proceedings.

"We can go to the back office," the man said. "The name's George – I'm the manager here."

A police tape had been placed in front of one of the entrances to the bowls club. DI Peters had been quick to seal off the scene. PC Woodbine was standing sentry in front of it. The giant man nodded a greeting to DS Skinner and DC Stone.

"Is that where he was found?" DC Stone pointed to the door behind the tape.

"That's where the changing rooms are," George said. "Follow me. My office is just through here."

He led them down a corridor and stopped outside a door on the left. He pushed it open and asked the two detectives to take a seat.

"Can you run through the series of events today?" DS Skinner said.

"Where do you want me to start?" George asked him.

"When was the last time you saw Benjamin?" DC Stone said. "Before you found him in the changing rooms I mean."

"He'd injured himself during the tenth end in the second game," George said. "So he decided to sit out the remaining ends."

"How on earth did he get injured playing bowls?" DC Stone wondered.

George laughed a hearty laugh. "It's more common than you'd think. Pulled muscles are the most common – that's what happened to Benjamin. And we had one member who was out for a whole season with a hernia. Bowls isn't for sissies, young man."

"Where did Benjamin go after he retired from the game?" DS Skinner said.

"He said he was going to get changed," George replied.

"What time was this?" DC Stone said.

"Probably around two. Yes, that would be about right. The match began at noon, and it was during the second game that Benjamin pulled a muscle."

"Didn't you think it odd that he didn't return to the green?" DS Skinner said.

"Not at all. He said he was going home, and I assumed he'd changed and done just that. Until I got the phone call from Jane, that is."

"And you went to look for him?"

"By then I was quite concerned," George said. "I know Benjamin, and I know he would have informed his wife if he was planning on stopping off for something on the way home."

"You found him in the changing rooms," DC Stone said. "Was that the first place you looked?"

"What are you implying?"

"My colleague isn't implying anything, George," DS Skinner said. "Unfortunately, we have to ask these questions."

"It was the logical assumption to make," George said. "There aren't many places to hide around here, and therefore there weren't many places Benjamin could have been if he was still at the club."

"Did you notice anyone hanging around the club earlier?" DS Skinner asked. "Someone who looked out of place. A non-member perhaps?"

"I don't recall seeing anyone strange," George said. "Although my mind was more on the game we were playing. We were up against the Richmond Rovers and there's always been a fierce rivalry between us."

"We're going to need a list of everybody who was here today," DC Stone said. "Members, staff, everybody."

"I can tell you right now that nobody at this club did that to Benjamin."

"We'll need that list, nevertheless," DS Skinner said.

"Did you see what they did to him?" George said.

"We haven't seen the body yet," DC Stone said.

"And you don't want to. That was barbaric. Who would do such a thing?"

"We'll find out," DS Skinner said. "I'm going to need you to come into the station to make a formal statement. I'm afraid it's standard procedure at times like these."

"I understand," George said. "And I'll do anything I can to help. Whoever did that to Benjamin needs locking up forever."

"We won't take up much more of your time."

"When will the club be able to open again? The giant in uniform told me there will be no more games until the police are finished. When exactly will that be?"

"I can't give you an answer to that," DS Skinner said. "It depends how long the forensics officers take to go over the scene."

"It's just it's Saturday tomorrow, and we've got a big tournament on. Do you think they'll be finished by tomorrow?"

"Probably," DS Skinner said. "Although I can't promise

anything. Thank you for your time. One of the uniforms will be speaking to you to arrange a convenient time for you to come over to St Peter Port to make that statement."

CHAPTER TWENTY SIX

"Benjamin Dodds was beaten repeatedly with a bowls ball."
Once again, O'Reilly was finding it difficult to digest what DI Peters had told him. The Head of Forensics suspected that Benjamin had been attacked from behind and he also believed the attack carried on long after his heart had stopped beating.

"Dr Lille will be able to confirm it," O'Reilly continued. "But Jim Peters thinks Mr Dodds was hit on the head again and again. He was probably taken by surprise and hit on the back of the head. The force of the blow will have probably knocked him unconscious, but whoever did this didn't stop there. The amount of blood on and around the body suggests this was a particularly vicious attack. There wasn't much left of his face."

DC Stone shivered. "What kind of sicko are we dealing with?"

"Someone who isn't averse to extreme violence,

Andy," O'Reilly said. "The bowls ball used to kill Mr Dodds was retrieved from the scene."

"I wonder why they left it behind," DC Stone said. "In the other murders the weapons used were taken away."

"A bowls ball is a bit tricky to hide under your coat," DC Owen said. "It would stick out like a sore thumb."

"Did Forensics get anything from the ball?" DS Skinner asked.

"It's still early days," O'Reilly said. "But DI Peters will make it a priority."

"Do we believe Benjamin Dodds's murder to be connected to the others?" DCI Fish said.

"They're connected," O'Reilly confirmed. "The MO with Benjamin's murder was different to how Harold Green and John Hillman were dispatched in that he wasn't killed at home, but they're connected, nevertheless. What do we know so far?"

"Whoever killed Benjamin knew his routine," DC Owen said.

"Right," O'Reilly said. "According to Mrs Dodds, Benjamin has played bowls every Friday for years. Our killer was aware of this."

"How many people would know he played bowls on a Friday?" DS Skinner said.

"James Green and Sasha Hillman would probably know about it," DC Owen said. "They live on the same street, and they would have seen him coming and going."

"Do we know where the kids were at the time of the attack?" DCI Fish asked.

"It was the first thing I checked," O'Reilly told him. "And unfortunately both the teenagers were at school. More than one teacher can confirm it."

"And Theresa Green is still in custody," DC Stone pointed out. "Which means we're looking for someone we haven't considered yet."

"That's right, Andy," O'Reilly agreed. "But I'm still convinced James and Sasha are involved somehow."

"How, Liam?" DCI Fish said. "Neither have them can be linked to any of the murders. How exactly are they involved?"

"I don't know," O'Reilly said. "I just get the feeling that they know something about all of this."

"Can I make a suggestion?" DCI Fish said.

"You're the superior officer in the room, Tom," O'Reilly said. "You can make all the suggestions you like."

"I'll pretend I didn't hear that. I would suggest that we waste no more time speculating on whether or not a pair of teenagers are involved in a triple murder and focus on what we know is fact."

"I'm all ears," O'Reilly said. "What do you suggest we focus on? Where do we go from here?"

"I'm inclined to agree with you regarding the connection between the three men based on their addresses. Men from three adjoining houses in a single street have been murdered, but we need to concentrate on why this is. What possible reason could there be to want these three men dead? In a collective sense, where is the motive here? We can see the motivation when we isolate the slayings – murder for money is an age-old motive, but we have nothing to suggest how anyone might gain from the deaths of all three of them."

O'Reilly opened his mouth to speak but no words came out.

He found his tongue a moment later. "The answer lies beyond the realms of reason."

Everyone in the room turned to look in his direction.

"Is that an old Irish idiox?" DC Stone dared.

"Idiom, you idiot," O'Reilly said. "And no, it isn't. Somewhere out there are the answers we seek, but until we know where they're hidden, we're blind. We're scrambling around in the dark."

"You're not making any sense, Liam," DCI Fish said.

"Nothing about this investigation has made sense," O'Reilly said. "Nothing. Somebody on this island stands to gain considerably with the three dead men out of the picture. This is about money – it's been about money from the onset, so that's where our focus has to be. Something links those three men together – something huge, and once we find out what that is, we'll be close to putting this one to bed."

"Where do you suggest we start looking?" DC Stone said.

"The devil's in the detail, Andy. We need to prepare ourselves for a mountain of grunt work. A veritable Mount Everest of drudgery."

"I'm not following you, sir."

"Documentation, Andy," O'Reilly explained. "Paperwork. We dig and we keep digging. In my experience, you dig deep enough you eventually stumble across what you're looking for. The motivation behind these murders will become clear in time – we just have to persevere. I want access to everything those dead men left behind. I want to see every insurance policy - every Last Will and Testament, and I want to know where their substantial wealth will end up in the event of their demise. That's where the answers lie in this investigation. There is at least one more player in this, and the identity of that player will be somewhere in that mountain of paperwork."

CHAPTER TWENTY SEVEN

"Is everything alright, Liam?"
DCI Fish was standing in the doorway of O'Reilly's office. The Irish detective had outlined what he needed everybody to do and left the briefing room without further explanation.

"Everything's grand, Tom," he said. "I just needed some clean air to clear my head a bit."
"You do realise that what you've suggested won't be easy," DCI Fish said. "We're talking warrants, subpoenas and the like, and that's going to take time."
"It is what it is. Someone stands to gain considerably from the deaths of these men, and that someone will be named in the small print somewhere. I want to know what contracts are in place – I want to know if there are any peculiar bequests and I want full access to everything pertaining to the result of these men ceasing to be."

DCI Fish took a seat opposite O'Reilly. "What about the kids? What are your plans with the teenagers?"

"We'll bring them in," O'Reilly said. "And we'll interview them both, but I think it might be a good idea to let them stew for a while."

"How long are you talking about?"

"It's Saturday tomorrow. Let's see how they like being hauled into a police interview on a weekend. James Green and Sasha Hillman are involved in this. We know they took no part in the murders, but they're inadvertently involved."

"I'm worried about Ann," DCI Fish changed the subject.

O'Reilly wasn't expecting it. "Tom?"

"She's been acting very odd," DCI Fish elaborated. "One minute she's like an affectionate schoolgirl and the next she's telling me not to touch her. Asking me how I can stand to be near a fat blob."

O'Reilly smiled.

"It's not funny, Liam," DCI Fish said. "It's starting to scare me."

"You're not the only man who's been subjected to this, Tom," O'Reilly said. "The mood swings get worse as the hormones change in preparation for giving birth."

"Are you saying it's perfectly normal?"

"It's perfectly normal," O'Reilly humoured him. "It doesn't last forever, and you'll find that once the baby is born it gets ten times worse."

"That is not very reassuring."

"I'm kidding with you," O'Reilly said. "Once that little Fish pops out, you'll be so busy running on autopilot you won't have time to notice anything else."

"Was it like that before your daughter was born? Did your wife have wild mood swings?"

"My Mary had wild mood swings before Assumpta was even thought about," O'Reilly said. "Irish women are famous for it. There's no need to worry about any of it. You'll both be fine. It'll all be forgotten about when the baby arrives. You don't know the sex, do you?"

"We didn't want to know, but I'm starting to wonder if we made a mistake there. It might be nice to prepare myself for the prospect of having another female in the house. I'm not sure I'll be able to cope with two of the unpredictable creatures."

"You'll cope," O'Reilly assured him. "I don't know about you but I'm knackered, and my brain is starting to shut down for the day."

"It is rather late," DC Fish said. "Let's call it a day. We'll make a start bright and early tomorrow."

He got to his feet. "Thank you for the chat. I

appreciate it."

"No problem," O'Reilly said. "You'll be alright. You and the Super will make great parents."

* * *

DI Peters was extremely confused. The Head of Forensics was a man of science and he trusted in that science implicitly. In his experience forensic evidence didn't lie. Fingerprints, fibres and DNA always told the truth. A spatter of blood wasn't capable of deception, nor did a ballistics fingerprint on the cartridge of a projectile ever spin a yarn, so why was the evidence he was looking at right now telling him something that could not possibly be true?

He'd checked it and checked it again and come to the same conclusion. The evidence was telling lies. For the first time ever in his career DI Peters was experiencing doubts about the reliability of his science. The bowls ball that he believed to have been used to kill Benjamin Dodds was staring at him from the table in the lab. It was taunting him with its secrets.

DI Peters had deduced that this was definitely the object used to inflict the fatal blows. The blood and fragments of bone lodged in the surface confirmed this. The cranial matter and the pieces of flesh stuck to the ball left no doubt about what had happened, but the fingerprints found on both sides of the ball were what was the most baffling.

The experienced forensics officer had reconstructed what he believed to have occurred with another bowls ball of similar size. DS Henry Earle had played the victim and DC Glenda Taylor had watched, amused as DI Peters had come at DS Earle from behind and mimicked bashing the back of his head in. The perpetrator would have had to hold the ball with two hands to carry out this kind of attack. A bowls ball is heavy and awkward to manoeuvre using just one hand, so DI Peters decided the killer had brought it down on the back of Benjamin Dodds's head with a hand on either side of the ball. The follow-up frenzy of blows had also been carried out with the killer holding onto the ball with both hands.

And the pattern of the fingerprints had corresponded to this. Two almost perfect sets of prints were pulled from either side of the bowls ball. This in itself was surprising. It was very careless of the killer to leave such glaring evidence behind, but when DI Peters analysed the prints in more detail, the results he came up with didn't make any sense whatsoever.

The fingerprints were on file. They were on file because they came from someone already involved in the investigation. They were Theresa Green's fingerprints. All the evidence pulled from the murder weapon pointed to a woman who was in police custody while the murder was carried out.

CHAPTER TWENTY EIGHT

O'Reilly thanked DC Stone for the lift and walked up the path towards his apartment. A cat meowed close by. O'Reilly turned to see a slim, ginger tom peering at him from the bushes next to the path.
"Fuck off."

It was the cat belonging to his neighbour. O'Reilly remembered how the ginger brute had tried to make a play for Juliet earlier in the year. Bram was having none of it and he told the neighbour's cat as much. O'Reilly also recalled how the neighbour had called him to complain about his cats' behaviour.
"Feck off," he said, and raised his stick in the air. "If you know what's good for you, you'll make yourself scarce."

"You there."
The voice came from the garden of the apartment next door.
"What do you think you're playing at?"
O'Reilly carried on walking towards his front door.
"I saw what you did there."

O'Reilly took a few deep breaths. He wasn't in the

mood for a confrontation with a pedantic little man right now.

"I could report you to the RSPCA for that."

O'Reilly looked him in the eye. "For what?"

"Abusing an animal. You were about to attack my Timothy with your stick. I could report you for that."

"I'll bear that in mind," O'Reilly said. "Will there be anything else?"

"I'll be keeping an eye on you."

O'Reilly started to laugh. He couldn't help it.

"This isn't funny. If it isn't bad enough that your two thugs never stop traumatising my little Timothy, now he has to contend with a mad Irishman with a stick. I know my rights."

"Grand," O'Reilly said and opened the door to his apartment.

Bram and Juliet were waiting for him by the front door. O'Reilly wondered if they'd heard the altercation outside.

"Evening, thugs," he said. "I imagine you'll be hungry."

He decided to treat them to something nice. They'd earned it. It was quite clear from the conversation with the neighbour that they'd been giving poor little Timothy a hard time and O'Reilly was proud of them. He opened two tins of tuna and filled their bowls. Bram and Juliet polished off the lot in less than a minute.

It was just after seven and O'Reilly had time for a shower and a beer before he had to set off for the Red Snapper. He was really looking forward to it. Meeting Victoria would be a welcome distraction from the investigation, and he decided he would try to put it out of his mind for at least one evening. The sound of his ringtone told him that wasn't going to be an option.

It was DI Peters. The Head of Forensics rarely phoned O'Reilly after hours and he had no option but to take the call – it had to be important.

"Jim," he said. "What have you found?"

"Something I can't explain," DI Peters said. "Theresa Green, I assume she's still in custody."

"That's right. We're still waiting on the CPS, but it's looking like we'll get the go ahead to charge her for the murder of her husband. For what it's worth – she didn't do it."

"I'm inclined to agree with you. Her prints were on the bowls ball used to kill Benjamin Dodds."

O'Reilly thought about this for a moment.

"I see," he said. "The killer has fucked up here, hasn't he?"

"Sorry?"

"No," O'Reilly said. "I'm sorry. Excuse my language. I think Theresa Green was set up for the murder of Harold, and I also think the golf club used to kill John Hillman was planted in the panic room to implicate her in that murder too. But it was careless to try and make it look like she was involved in the murder at the bowls club when Mrs Green was locked up at the time."

"I'm just going on the forensic evidence," DI Peters said.

"How did they do it?" O'Reilly wondered. "How did they get her prints onto the murder weapons?"

"It's not difficult," DI Peters said. "They could have used the same process we use to transfer prints for analysis. All it takes is a basic knowledge of operational forensics. You find a surface with clear prints on it, retrieve them with adhesive tape then transfer them onto another surface."

"Have you ever come across this before?"

"Not in a professional capacity," DI Peters said. "But I've read about it in a few crime thrillers."

"I didn't know you were a fan of crime fiction."

"Always have been. I know – it's a bit of a busman's holiday sort of thing, but they actually help me to wind down. What do you suggest we do with this evidence, Liam?"

"This is a real breakthrough," O'Reilly said. "Whoever did this really slipped up. Someone has gone to great lengths to get Theresa Green out of the picture, but this has actually worked against them. We now have clear evidence that she was set up for the murder of Benjamin Dodds, and we can use that to prove the same thing applies to the death of her husband. This might even be enough to give her a get out of jail free card. Thanks for letting me know."

They said their goodbyes and O'Reilly fetched a beer from the fridge. He realised he was smiling. The phone call from DI Peters had cheered him up a bit. This was the first mistake the killer had made, and O'Reilly knew from experience that when they reached that point often more blunders followed. He drained the beer and went to take a quick shower.

CHAPTER TWENTY NINE

Victoria wasn't there when O'Reilly arrived at the Red Snapper. He assumed she was just running late. He asked the waiter for a table for two and was led to one of the tables by the window. He ordered a beer and took a look around while the waiter went to get it. The restaurant was busy and there were only a few tables free. O'Reilly had stumbled upon the Red Snapper in his first week on the island and it was a place he always came back to. The food was delicious, and they also served his favourite beer. The *Scapegoat* not only tasted great O'Reilly was drawn to the name of it. It was a fitting beer for a police detective to drink.

The waiter came back with the beer and two menus. O'Reilly thanked him and took out his phone to see if there were any messages from Victoria. It wasn't like her to be late. There was nothing on his phone to explain why she wasn't there yet. O'Reilly took a long drink of his beer and smiled. He'd really acquired a taste for the local brew, and he was glad he'd found it.

A familiar face caught his attention and O'Reilly nodded to the huge man at the back of the restaurant. The man smiled and made his way over to O'Reilly's table.
"It's nice to see you again."
Bertram Pink was the head chef at the Red Snapper and O'Reilly had grown to like him. He'd had his share

of drama in the past, but he'd bounced back remarkably well and O'Reilly respected him for that.

"It's great to see you too," he said.

"Are you dining alone?" Bertram asked.

"I'm waiting for Victoria. She's running late."

"A woman's prerogative."

"Is there anything you can recommend this evening?" O'Reilly said.

"That depends what you're in the mood for. If you feel like something from the sea, I can give you an insider tip. The calamari is as fresh as it gets, and I prepare it with a new sauce I've developed."

"Sounds like a good option."

"Or," Bertram continued. "If you're in the mood for something bloody and meaty, the fillet steak is always a winner."

"I get enough blood and meat at work," O'Reilly informed him. "I think I'll opt for the seafood."

"I can highly recommend the platter for two then."

"I'll wait for Victoria before I decide," O'Reilly said.

"No problem," Bertram said. "It's really great to see you again."

Victoria arrived ten minutes later. She apologised for being late before sitting down at the table.

"The bike wouldn't start," she explained. "I've been meaning to replace the battery, but I never got round to it. I had to call a cab."

"You're here now," O'Reilly said. "What would you like to drink?"

"Water will be fine."

O'Reilly caught the attention of the waiter and ordered the water.

"How have you been?" he asked.

"Bored," she said. "Even though I've managed to persuade Tommy to let me work half day at the shop I'm going spare at home. There's nothing wrong with me."

O'Reilly raised an eyebrow.

"Don't, Liam," she warned. "I've been feeling fine. It took a while to get used to the side-effects of the radiation treatment, but I'm working through it. The doctor explained that it affects people in different ways, and it appears I'm one of the lucky ones."

"You don't want to overdo it."

"I'm not allowed to overdo it," Victoria said.

"And that's probably why you're feeling OK. What else has the doctor said?"

"The cancer hasn't spread," Victoria told him. "Which is good news. Can we talk about something else?

What's been happening in your life?"

"Stuff we really shouldn't be discussing over dinner. Let's talk about something pleasant instead."

"Wedding talk it is then."

"I said something *pleasant*," O'Reilly dared.

"Liam."

O'Reilly held up his hands. "Go on then. What's on your mind?"

The waiter came back with Victoria's water and asked them if they were ready to order. O'Reilly asked him to give them another five minutes.

"I was thinking about an autumn wedding," Victoria said. "Late September."

"That works for me," O'Reilly said. "The weather is still warm, and it doesn't rain much at that time of year."

"I've been looking at some possible venues. I've had a lot of free time on my hands."

"Venues for what?"

"The reception of course."

"Don't we have to get married first?" O'Reilly said.

"Before we head to the reception."

"We can do that at a registry office. With a few witnesses present. Tommy and Assumpta perhaps."

"I thought you would want a big fancy do," O'Reilly said. "Horse and carriage and the whole hog."

"I'm not a fairytale kind of girl. We're not a couple of kids, Liam and neither of us is particularly religious either."

"Me and God had a bit of a falling out a few years ago," O'Reilly admitted. "Registry office it is then. Where did you have in mind for the reception?"

"I've narrowed it down to two places. Both of them are in Vazon."

"It's not going to be cheap then."

"I'll pretend you didn't say that," Victoria said and took a sip of her water. "The one I'm leaning towards at the moment is the Bay Hotel up in Albecq. It's overlooking the beach, and they have a wonderful garden there."

"I'm happy with whatever you choose," O'Reilly said. "It's your day."

"It's our day. I want you to be involved."

"And I will. What do you feel like eating?"

CHAPTER THIRTY

They ordered the food, and the waiter informed them it would be about half an hour. Victoria opted for the fillet steak with the pepper sauce and O'Reilly decided to push the boat out and order a seafood platter for two. He was advised that the details were in the name, and it was far too much food for one person to eat, to which the Irishman had replied with just two words.

"Challenge accepted."

"I've never come across anyone with an appetite like yours," Victoria said when the waiter had finished taking their order.

"I've always had a thing for food," he told her. "And that brings us to the next thing on the agenda. What are we going to feed the masses at the wedding reception?"

"It'll hardly be masses. I don't know how many people you'll be inviting, but my list totals just over twenty people."

"I don't think I know twenty people," O'Reilly said. "I'll give it some thought."

"Will you be inviting anyone from home?"

"Guernsey is home now. And I doubt anyone I invited would make the trip out from Ireland just to watch me get married."

"Make out a list," Victoria said. "You might just surprise yourself."

"I suppose I ought to invite the team from work."

"Definitely. You're a close working group, and you can't leave anyone out."

The food arrived and when the waiter put down his

seafood platter O'Reilly wondered if he'd bitten off more than he could chew. He wondered if he ought to admit defeat and tell the waiter he wasn't quite up to the challenge. The platter was huge. There were prawns, scallops, crab, calamari, mussels and a whole fillet of fish. A portion of chips was also included on the plate.

"Good luck, sir," the waiter said with a wink.

That was all the encouragement O'Reilly needed, and he tucked in.

"Are you going to eat that?" Victoria asked twenty minutes later.

She pointed to O'Reilly's plate. A solitary prawn was all that remained.

O'Reilly rubbed his belly. "Be my guest. I'm stuffed."

Victoria laughed and helped herself to the prawn.

"That has to be some kind of a record. I bet you'd be a real hit at an all you can eat buffet."

"I got banned from a few places back in Dublin," O'Reilly told her. "My name was actually up on a board in one restaurant."

"I can believe that. This has been nice."

"It has," O'Reilly agreed. "After the day I've had it's been just what the doctor ordered."

"I read about the *Death Rue* thing."

"The Herald have outdone themselves this time. Fred Viking never ceases to amaze me."

"It really does beggar belief though," Victoria said. "Three men in the same street. Do you know what it's all about?"

"Money. It's as simple as that, but the actual motivation is proving to be elusive. We'll get there in the end."

"You always do. I don't suppose you'll be ordering dessert."

"Give me ten minutes," O'Reilly said. "And I'll let you know."

Bertram Pink came over to the table. He had a four-pack of *Scapegoat* in his hand. He placed it on the table and patted O'Reilly on the back.

"What's this?" the Irishman asked.

"Call it first prize in the seafood eating contest," Bertram said. "That was quite a feat. David has talked about nothing else since he cleared your plates away."

O'Reilly looked at the beers. "That's really not necessary."

"Call it public relations. I trust the platter was to your liking."

"It was delicious."

"The fillet steak was the best I've ever tasted,"

Victoria added. "Compliments to the chef."

Bertram laughed. "I'll let him know."

"I think you have a fan," Victoria said when the giant head chef had gone back to the kitchen.

"I like him," O'Reilly said. "And I helped him get through a tough spot a while ago. He's a good man."

"*You're* a good man, Liam O'Reilly. And I can't wait to be your wife."

"How does Tommy feel about it?" O'Reilly asked. "I haven't really given much thought to how your big brother feels about having a grumpy Irishman as a brother-in-law."

"Tommy is just Tommy. Nobody will ever be good enough for his little sister. He likes you really. He's just got a funny way of showing it. There's something else we need to discuss."

"Sounds serious."

"Not really," Victoria said. "We need to talk about where we're going to live after we're married."

"I hadn't given it much thought."

"We can't carry on living on opposite sides of the island. That would be just weird."

"What did you have in mind?" O'Reilly asked.

"Your job is here in the capital," Victoria said. "And the bike shop is over in Vazon, so the practical thing to do would be to meet in the middle. Somewhere like Beaucamps, perhaps."

"But that would mean you selling your house. You love that house."

"And you would be moving out of your apartment."

"It wouldn't bother me in the slightest," O'Reilly said. "It's just an apartment. And my neighbour is really starting to irritate me with his whining about his poor Timothy."

"What are you suggesting?"

"I move in with you."

"In Vazon?"

"Unless you have another property hidden away," O'Reilly said. "It's a ten-minute commute across the island to the Island Police HQ. I'll be allowed to drive again soon, and it wouldn't put me out at all. It used to be a forty-five -minute slog through traffic to get to work back in Dublin."

"Are you sure?"

"I am. As long as Tommy is happy about it, I mean. It was his house too at one stage."

"It's all mine now," Victoria said. "Tommy wasn't interested in it."

"We can come to some arrangement with splitting the costs," O'Reilly said. "You own the house, so it's only right that I pay for everything else."

"When we're married, what's mine is yours and what's yours is mine. Half of the house will belong to you then."

"I don't want that," O'Reilly said. "The house is yours. It will stay yours even when we're married. I'm not a materialistic man. It'll be simpler that way. We can even put something down on paper. Some kind of contract."

"Like a pre-nup?"

"Whatever it takes. It's your house, and I have no right to it."

"I love you, Liam."

"And I love you. But you also seem to be forgetting about the baggage I'll be bringing with me."

"I'm sure my lady can tolerate another two cats in the house."

"That's that then," O'Reilly said. "I'll let the landlord know I'll be moving out soon."

CHAPTER THIRTY ONE

O'Reilly was woken the next morning by an ungodly screech. He shot up in bed and everything was silent. A few seconds passed and he heard it again. It sounded like it was right outside his window. He got up and opened the curtains. Two ginger toms were facing off in the garden. The hair on Bram's back was standing straight up, and he was baring his teeth. O'Reilly had never seen him look so feral. He really did resemble a wild thing.

Bram's display seemed to do the trick. The cat O'Reilly knew was called Timothy backed off and darted into the undergrowth between the two apartments.

"That's my boy," O'Reilly said.

He wondered if he would get another visit from the petty neighbour. He decided that if he did, he would use Bram as an example. He went to the bathroom and looked at his reflection in the mirror. He bared his teeth, but it didn't quite have the same effect as Bram's show of dominance.

He made some tea and took it outside to the small garden. It was not yet seven, but it was already very warm and it promised to be another glorious day on the island. O'Reilly sat down on one of the chairs around the table and thought back to the conversation with Victoria in the Red Snapper. He hadn't given it a second thought when he'd agreed to move in with her in Vazon, and only now were the implications of that starting to take hold. He was starting to realise how complicated things became when money and property was involved. He decided the marriage to Victoria would be free from those sort of complications. The house would remain in her name, and they could start their new life together in a simple fashion.

Something occurred to O'Reilly during the walk to work. It was something that he hadn't dwelled upon earlier but in light of the recent developments between himself and Victoria Radcliffe it was brought to the surface. He recalled the conversation with Jane Dodds yesterday and something she'd mentioned came back to him. Jane told him her house had been sold, and she also said the lawyer came round earlier with the papers for her to sign. O'Reilly realised this was quite odd. Jane had used the possessive determiner *my* when she'd spoken about the house. She was the one who'd signed the papers pertaining to the sale of the house. This could only mean one thing: Jane was the sole owner of number 6 Rue La Mere.

O'Reilly turned onto La Grange and instead of taking the road that led to the station he carried on walking until he reached the beach road. Something was bothering him, and he needed some sea air to help him to clear up what it was that was niggling at his insides. He stepped onto the sand and made his way towards the sea. It was still early but a few people were already enjoying the morning sun on the beach.

O'Reilly stopped a few metres from the surf and looked out to sea. The island of Herm seemed bigger today, and there were more boats out on the water than usual. Summer had arrived on the island. O'Reilly wondered what it was about Jane Dodds's words that had stirred something up in his insides. Why was the fact that she was the owner of the house so important?

It came to him while gazing out at a sailboat close to the shore. If Jane Dodds was the deeds holder of number 6 why was Benjamin murdered? So far, they'd assumed that the motive in the murders was plain and simple. Arnold Green and John Hillman were probably killed for money, but what would anyone stand to gain by murdering a man who didn't have any? There was no reason to want Benjamin Dodds dead. The whole thing was bugging him, and O'Reilly decided it would be the first thing on the agenda in the morning briefing.

The walk back up to the station took longer than usual because of a strange encounter with a man O'Reilly had never met before. It was clear from the urgency of the man's stride as he approached that he knew exactly who O'Reilly was. He strode with purpose and for a split-second O'Reilly actually braced himself for an attack.

The man didn't attack the Irish detective. Instead, he introduced himself as Rupert Nunn and extended his hand. O'Reilly found himself shaking it.

"You don't know me," Rupert said. "But I know you. I've seen you in the papers."

"I didn't realise I was famous," O'Reilly said.

"This is a small island."

"Is there something I can help you with?"

"It's more a case of me helping you. I was at the bowls club yesterday when Benjamin was murdered."

O'Reilly was suddenly very interested.

"Do you have some information for me?"

"I spoke to one of your lot at the club yesterday," Rupert told him. "But he didn't seem interested in what I had to say. If you ask me, you shouldn't have people like that in the Island Police."

"Who did you talk to?"

"His name escapes me, but you couldn't miss him. Giant of a man. All bulk and no brains if you ask me."

PC Woodbine then, O'Reilly decided.

"What is it you wanted to tell me?" he asked.

"I saw someone at the club yesterday," Rupert said.

"Someone who shouldn't have been there."

"How do you know they shouldn't have been there?"

"Because I've been at the club since the beginning. I know everyone there, and by that, I mean everyone."

"What was this stranger doing?" O'Reilly said.

"Lingering. That's all they were doing – lingering."

"Where was this?"

"Over by the changing rooms."

"I haven't been to the bowls club," O'Reilly said.

"Could you explain the set-up there?"

"The green is on the west side. Then there's a pavilion and behind that is the clubhouse. The changing rooms are to the right of that."

"Can you describe this person?" O'Reilly said.

"He was wearing one of those hooded top things," Rupert said. "That's when I knew he was up to no good."

"Did you see his face?"

"He had his back to me."

"How do you know it was a man?" O'Reilly asked.

"Simple deduction."

"Could you explain what you mean by that?"

"It's basic logic. If the person I saw was the one who killed Benjamin it had to have been a man. George told me what happened to the poor guy, and I know for a fact that no woman is capable of that."

"I see. Was there anything else about this person you remember?"

"I only saw him for a moment," Rupert said. "Then the second game started, and my attention was drawn elsewhere."

"Benjamin was injured during that game, wasn't he?"

"He pulled a muscle and had to be substituted."

"And you didn't see the stranger again?" O'Reilly said. "You didn't see him after Benjamin left the green?"

"No. We carried on with the game. We won by the way. We were just packing up the bowls when all hell broke loose. That's when George found poor Benjamin."

O'Reilly glanced at his watch. He was late for the morning briefing.

"I'd like you to come to the station and put what you've just told me on record. Can you do that?"

"Will there be some kind of reward?" Rupert said. "If my information helps you catch the monster who did that to Benjamin I mean."

"That's not how we work," O'Reilly informed him. "But we would be very grateful for any information."

"I'll come in during the course of the day. Can I go now?"

It was you who accosted me, O'Reilly thought, but kept it to himself.

"Of course. Thank you for the information."

CHAPTER THIRTY TWO

Even though he was already late for the morning meeting, O'Reilly made himself a cup of tea first. He took it with him to the briefing room.

"Sorry I'm late. I got held up talking to a witness from the bowls club. Rupert Nunn. He claims he saw someone hanging around the changing rooms yesterday."

"Why didn't he tell this to the officers on the scene?" DCI Fish wondered.

"Apparently he did," O'Reilly said. "He spoke to PC Woodbine about it, but he got the impression he wasn't taken seriously."

"Could he give you a description of this person?" DS Skinner said.

"A very vague one. He said the stranger was wearing a hoodie, and he didn't see the face. He's convinced it's a man because he reckons a woman isn't capable of that level of brutality."

"Interesting," DCI Fish said.

"I told him to come in to make a statement. For what it's worth. He didn't give me much."

"He might remember more when he's questioned," DC Stone said. "He might be able to give us some idea of the height and build."

"Right," O'Reilly said. "Before we get down to business, I want to get the ball rolling with the release of Theresa Green."

"What?" It was DCI Fish.

"She didn't kill her husband, Tom. I think she was telling the truth when she said she was over in Herm. She was set up. DI Peters phoned me yesterday to tell me about something he found. Theresa's prints were on the bowls ball used to kill Benjamin Dodds."

"But that's impossible," DC Stone said.

"The killer slipped up, Andy. I believe she was framed for the murder of Arnold Green and John Hillman, and she was supposed to take the rap for the brutal slaying of Benjamin Dodds, but she has the best alibi there is for that one."

"How did her prints end up on the bowls ball?" DC Owen said.

"It's easier than you think, Katie. You pull some prints with a piece of tape and transfer them straight onto another surface. I believe that's how her fingerprints ended up on the knife we found in her car too."

"Unbelievable," DCI Fish exclaimed.

"Indeed," O'Reilly agreed. "And that's why we need to get Theresa Green released as soon as possible. She's done nothing wrong, and I can't sit by and watch an innocent woman have her freedom taken away."

"Are you absolutely sure about this, Liam?" DCI Fish asked.

"As sure as buggery, Tom. The prints on the bowls ball all but put her in the clear for the murder of her husband."

"I'll put our findings to the CPS," DCI Fish said. "It's not going to be a quick process though."

"As long as she's released as soon as possible," O'Reilly said.

"If the CPS believe her to be innocent, she will be released."

"If her prints were transferred to the bowls ball," DC Stone said. "It has to be someone close to her. How else would someone be able to obtain a set of her fingerprints?"

"Of course it's someone close to her, Andy," O'Reilly said. "You don't go around framing complete strangers for murder."

"I was just thinking out loud, sir."

"Something occurred to me this morning," O'Reilly carried on. "With regards to the murder of Benjamin Dodds. When we spoke to Mrs Dodds yesterday, she mentioned the sale of number 6 Rue La Mere."

"She said the house was far too big for just her and Benjamin," DC Owen remembered.

"When she talked about it, she said the lawyer had been there earlier so she could sign the paperwork."

"What has the sale of the house got to do with Mr Dodds's murder?" DC Stone said.

"She called it *my* house, Andy," O'Reilly said. "She was the one who signed the papers. I remember when my wife and I sold our first house. Both of us had to put our signatures on the paperwork."

"Are you saying Mrs Dodds is the sole owner of the house?" DCI Fish said.

"I am."

"Then why was Benjamin murdered?" DC Owen said. "If this has been about money all along, why murder someone who doesn't appear to have any assets?"

"My thoughts exactly, Katie," O'Reilly said. "What is the reason behind killing Benjamin? That was a particularly brutal murder, and it was extremely risky carrying it out at the bowls club. It doesn't make any sense. Why take such a risk on a man who by all accounts has very little to offer?"

Nobody had an answer to this.

"Do we know for certain that Mrs Dodds is the deeds holder of the house?" DCI Fish said.

"It'll be easy to find out," O'Reilly said.

"How?"

"Ask the woman. Ask her if she is the sole owner of number 6 Rue La Mere."

"We've got her details," DC Owen said. "I'll give her a call."

She left the room and returned shortly afterwards. She nodded her head. "It's true. The only name on the title deeds of number 6 is Jane's."

"Why?" DS Skinner wondered. "They've been married for decades. Why is it she owns the house?"

"According to Mrs Dodds," DC Owen said. "It was done on the advice of Benjamin's father."

"Mr Dodds's dad advised her to do that?" DCI Fish said. "What on earth for?"

"Jane was very forthcoming, sir," DC Owen said.

"Benjamin's father warned Jane about her husband's business decisions. He'd made some bad ones and lost quite a bit of money in the process. Their marriage contract was a strange one. It meant that their assets weren't combined, and any debt Benjamin incurred wouldn't become Jane's problem."

"So the property was put in Jane's name only so the creditors couldn't touch it if it came to that?" DCI Fish supposed.

"I'm finding it hard to understand all this," DC Stone said.

"It's how the rich stay rich, Andy," O'Reilly said. "Us working class plebs wouldn't even think of doing something like that. It means that it doesn't matter how much debt someone runs up, the wolfs can't come around and touch the spouse. In Benjamin's case he knew his house would always be safe. But we're getting sidetracked here. It still doesn't explain why a man ended up getting his head bashed in with a bowls ball. Nobody stands to gain anything by doing that."

"I'm baffled," DS Skinner said. "I don't mind admitting it."

"What do we know about Benjamin's other finances?" DC Stone said. "It's possible he might have other assets."

"He must have money somewhere," DS Skinner said.

"He filed for bankruptcy a while ago, Sarge," DC Owen said. "According to Jane it was no secret. The man had nothing. Everything they had was legally owned by his wife."

"A kept man," DC Stone said. "Some blokes have all the luck."

"Never going to happen, Andy," O'Reilly said. "That is never going to happen to you."

"Where do you propose we go from here?" DCI Fish asked O'Reilly.

"Paperwork," he replied. "We need to delve into the finances of all three victims. We know Benjamin Dodds had bugger all, but Harold Green and John Hillman were considerably well off. Someone is going to inherit their assets, and that someone will be involved in this somehow."

"I don't get it, sir," DC Stone said. "How can Arnold and John's assets be connected? Unless there are more people involved than we think, I can't see how a single killer can benefit."

"And you're forgetting something else," DCI Fish said.

"You're insisting that Theresa Green be released as soon as possible. If that happens, she'll be entitled to the majority of her husband's wealth. Thirty million."

"It's a bit of a conundrum," O'Reilly said.

"Unless she really is involved," DC Owen put forward.

"Are you suggesting she framed herself for the murder of her husband?"

"That's ridiculous," DC Stone said. "And she can't possibly have murdered Benjamin Dodds. She was in custody at the time."

"There is definitely more than one person involved in this," O'Reilly insisted.

"And it is still possible that Theresa Green is one of them," DS Skinner joined in. "Let's look at it from another perspective. Outline a possible scenario. Mrs Green kills her husband. She drives to the tennis club and leaves the car there with the knife in the glove compartment. She knows it won't be long before we join the dots and she's arrested."

"What about John Hillman?" DC Stone said.

"Just bear with me, Andy. Mrs Green conveniently disappears off the face of the earth. She was AWOL at the time John Hillman was killed. Then she miraculously appears at the station because she's heard we're looking for her. She knows she's in deep trouble, and she knows she'll probably be locked up. That's when her accomplice puts the next part of the plan into action. Benjamin Dodds is murdered, and Theresa's prints are on the bowls ball used to kill him. But how is that possible? The woman was in police custody at the time. We put two and two together and presume she's been set up, and that makes us suspicious about the murder of her husband. Was she framed for that one too?"

"That's a valid scenario, Will," O'Reilly admitted. "But we still have no idea how Theresa is linked to John Hillman and Benjamin Green. What does she stand to gain from their deaths? Benjamin had nothing, and I doubt John will have left Theresa anything. She's going to be thirty million better off – why not leave it at that. Why kill two other unconnected men?"

"The only way to rule it out is to dig into the finances of all three families," DCI Fish said. "As you suggested."

"That's right," O'Reilly said. "That's precisely what we need to do."

CHAPTER THIRTY THREE

After taking a short break to get something to eat, the team got back to work. It had been an exhausting and somewhat unproductive morning, and O'Reilly was starting to wonder if it had been a mistake looking into the history of three families on a Saturday. The weekend really wasn't the best time to try and find out about a person's financial situation, and the majority of people they'd spoken to told them to call back on Monday.

DC Owen had suggested another approach. Perhaps they could dig something up from the Internet. O'Reilly agreed – that's what they would do after the break for lunch. Often the web was a treasure trove of information if you knew where to look. He wasn't very internet savvy so he left that task to the people on the team who were more au fait with the ins and outs of the world wide web, and he focused his attention elsewhere. He needed to speak to Theresa Green again. He got the feeling she hadn't told them everything and he needed to do something about that.

Sergeant Gough informed O'Reilly that Theresa was bearing up remarkably well. The duty sergeant told him she'd been very upbeat considering her predicament and this aroused suspicion in the Irishman. He knew that often not everything was as it seemed, and he felt that this was one of those times.

Theresa Green was escorted to one of the interview rooms and O'Reilly asked her to take a seat. He'd debated whether to conduct an official interview but decided not to. He would have a friendly chat with the women. Perhaps she would tell him more without the prying ears of the recording device distracting her.

Sergeant Gough hadn't been exaggerating when he said Theresa was bearing up well. She didn't look like someone who'd been arrested for the brutal murder of her husband. She seemed relaxed and her eyes were bright. O'Reilly didn't know how to read her. Either she was innocent, and she believed in the justice system enough to have faith that she would be released in time, or she was aware of the prints on the bowls ball, and she knew full well this would throw some doubt on her involvement in her husband's murder.

"This isn't a formal interview," O'Reilly informed her. "It's just a friendly chat. How are you?"

"Irritated," she said.

"I can appreciate that. You'll be happy to know that some new information has come to light. Some information that might help you."

"Are you telling me I'll be allowed to go home?"

"It's possible," O'Reilly said. "But I need to ask you a few more questions first."

"Fire away," Theresa said and smiled. "It's not like I get much social interaction in here."

"When we last spoke you mentioned something about your husband having an affair," O'Reilly said. "Could you elaborate on that."

"What is there to elaborate on? Arnold was knocking off the secretary of the golf club. There isn't much more to say."

"Who is this woman?"

"I would have thought that would be one of the first questions you'd ask."

"We've been otherwise engaged," O'Reilly said. "With more pressing matters."

"Hillary is her name," Theresa said. "Hillary Maddox."

"Which golf club is she secretary of?"

"Vazon. That's how Arnold met her."

"And that's the reason you told him to move out?"

"Do I need a better reason?"

"I suppose not," O'Reilly said.

"He's old enough to be her father," Theresa told him. "I suppose money can buy anything these days. Why are you suddenly so interested in that tart?"

"We're just covering all the bases. Arnold made you sign a pre-nuptial contract, is that correct?"

"You know it is."

"And you agreed?"

"What choice did I have?"

"I don't know. Do you know Benjamin Dodds well?"
This took her by surprise. "Excuse me?"
"Benjamin Dodds," O'Reilly said. "How well do you know him?"
"He lived at number 6."
O'Reilly looked her in the eyes. She held eye contact for a few seconds and looked away.
"Excuse me for a moment."
He got up and left the room without offering any further explanation.

"What's going on?" Theresa asked when he returned a few minutes later.
"Nothing to concern yourself with. Where were we? Benjamin Dodds."
"What about him. I barely spoke to the man. I would say hello to Jane, but Benjamin was a strange one."
"So, you didn't really associate with the Dodds's?"
"Not at all. Why are you asking me about Benjamin? You can't think I had anything to do with what happened to him."
"That's what's bothering me," O'Reilly said.
"In what way?"
"I don't know," O'Reilly said. "There's something not quite right. It might be nothing. How long have you lived on Rue La Mere?"

"Only a few years. We moved there in 2016 I think."

"Next door to the Hillman family?"

"Why are you asking questions you already know the answers to?"

"It's a bad habit of mine," O'Reilly said. "What do you think of Benjamin Dodds?"

"Why do you keep talking about him? I was banged up in here when he was killed. You know I was."

O'Reilly scratched his nose and his gaze fell on Theresa again.

"That's the problem," he said. "I've just spoken to the duty sergeant, and he informed me you've received no visitors, and you haven't requested any phone calls."

"What about it?" Theresa said.

"How did you know Benjamin was dead?"

There was a moment of silence in the room. Theresa frowned and her face broke out into a smile.

"How did you know Benjamin was dead?" O'Reilly asked her again.

"You told me."

"I most certainly did not," O'Reilly argued.

"You did. You spoke about him in the past tense, so I jumped to the assumption that he must be."

"I asked you three questions about him," O'Reilly reminded her. "I said *do you know Benjamin well* – I asked you what you think of him, and I also asked *how well do you know him*. Present tense in all three instances."

"I'm not saying anything else to you."

"That's your right," O'Reilly said. "But I would advise you not to go that route."

"No comment," Theresa said.

She folded her arms and grinned at O'Reilly, and he realised the conversation was over.

CHAPTER THIRTY FOUR

After popping in to check the progress of the team O'Reilly made his mind up to look elsewhere for answers. None of the detectives had come across anything relevant on the Internet. There was nothing about the three dead men that shed any light on a possible reason why they were killed. There wasn't anything about Arnold Green more than what O'Reilly had already read. He was born into money, and he'd managed to hold on to the majority of that money – end of story.

They learned that John Hillman ran a large IT company from the island. John was the CEO of a firm that specialised in cyber security. John and his IT specialists had designed software that was used in more than twenty countries across the globe. The HQ of the company was on the island, and all operations were carried out there. There wasn't much about John's actual worth, but one article did catch DC Owen's interest. Just over a year ago a rival IT operation had offered almost fifty million dollars for the company. John had declined the offer.

The only thing they could ascertain about Benjamin Dodds was he was an avid bowls player. There were photographs and write-ups about various tournaments on the island and abroad. There was no mention of what Benjamin did for work, and the more DS Skinner read the more he realised that he was a relatively unremarkable man. He'd lost a substantial amount of money in the nineties, but he appeared to have bounced back. DS Skinner assumed he had his wife to thank for this.

That was all they had so far. There was nothing on the Internet to help them get any real answers about why these three men had to die. DC Owen told O'Reilly as much.

"It was a long shot," he said. "Come on – we're heading over to Vazon."

"What's in Vazon?" she asked.

"Apart from a disgusting amount of money?" O'Reilly said. "There's a woman there who might be able to give us some more information about one of the dead men. Her name is Hillary Maddox, she works at the golf club, and she was having an affair with Arnold Green."

The Saturday afternoon traffic was sparce and they made it across the island in ten minutes.

"I'll be moving here soon, Katie," O'Reilly told DC Owen when they'd reached the turnoff in Castel.

"You're moving to Vazon?"

"It makes sense. Victoria asked me to move in with her after we get married."

"Wow," DC Owen said. "You'll be rubbing shoulders with the rich and famous then."

"Do I look like a man who gives a hoot about money?"

DC Owen laughed. "Not exactly, sir. When is the wedding? Have you set a date yet?"

"Sometime in September. Don't worry – you're invited."

"I'll look forward to it. Perhaps you ought to think about making it a double wedding. With Assumpta and

Andy."

"I used to like you, Katie Owen," O'Reilly said. "The golf club is just up here on the left. There was a sign for it back there."

They flashed their IDs at the man at the security gate and he instructed them to carry on down the lane and park in the designated area.

"Is Hillary expecting us?" DC Owen asked.

"Where's the fun in that," O'Reilly said. "I don't believe she's involved in this, but you can't be too careful."

DC Owen parked next to a black 4x4 and she and O'Reilly got out.

"Where's your stick, sir?" DC Owen asked.

"I've had a crutch for far too long, Katie," he said. "It's about time I stood on my own two feet. You'll have to bear with me though – it takes a bit longer to get around without it."

The club was busy. It was a glorious Saturday afternoon, and the place was buzzing with people. Golf carts were coming and going from the fairways and greens. Some of the players were on foot. Lugging golf bags behind them, they were getting some exercise in the sun.

"I can't see the point of this game," O'Reilly said.

"Me neither," DC Owen agreed. "Although I suppose it's a good way to get some fresh air and sunshine."

"I can think of better ways to do that. I assume this is the reception area."

He opened the door for DC Owen, and they went into the clubhouse. It was much cooler in here – the air conditioners were working well, and O'Reilly could feel the sweat cooling on his forehead. He spotted what looked like the reception desk and walked up to it.

"We're looking for Hillary," he said to a pretty woman who appeared to be in her mid-twenties. "Hillary Maddox."

She smiled at him. "You've found her. What can I do for you? Are you thinking of joining the club, because there's a waiting list."

"That's not why we're here," O'Reilly said and showed her his Island Police warrant card. "DI O'Reilly and this is DC Owen. Is there somewhere we can talk in private?"

"Is this about Arnold?"

"Can we talk somewhere in private?" O'Reilly asked her again.

She arranged for another woman to cover the front desk and led O'Reilly and DC Owen down a long corridor. She stopped outside a room with a sign on the door that read *Staff Only*.

"We won't be disturbed in here."

They sat round a small table.

"I couldn't believe it when I heard what had happened," Hillary said. "I'd only seen Arnold the previous evening. I assume that's why you're here."

"Was your relationship serious?" O'Reilly said.

"I know what you must be thinking."

"I assure you, you don't," O'Reilly said.

"Well, I know what everyone else thought. That I was only with Arnold for his money, but it was much more than that."

"I see. You said you were with him the evening before he died. Where was this?"

"At my apartment in Le Gele."

"Did he mention anything about paying a visit to the house on Rue La Mere?"

She shook her head. "He didn't mention anything to me about it."

"Can you think of why he would go to the house?" DC Owen said. "Perhaps he went to fetch some belongings."

"I told you," Hillary said. "He didn't say anything to me about it."

"How long have you known Arnold?" O'Reilly said.

"A few years," Hillary said. "I met him here at the club. He'd been a member for years."

"But I believe you only started your relationship with him a few months ago."

"It just happened. We've always got on, and he did used to flirt a bit, but it was all harmless fun."

"What changed?" DC Owen said.

"I don't know. I suppose he was having some problems with his marriage. It wasn't my fault. I'm not a homewrecker if that's what you're thinking." She looked straight at O'Reilly when she said this.

"I'll ask you to refrain from presuming what I'm thinking," he said. "If you don't mind."

"I'm sorry," Hillary said. "I'm just telling you that I wasn't to blame for the breakup of the marriage. That was already happening when Arnold and I got together."

"Do you know Mrs Green well?" O'Reilly asked.

"Theresa?" Hillary spat the word out. "Of course. She comes to the club every now and again."

"You don't like her?" DC Owen said.

"She's a stuck-up cow. She's the one you should be looking into if you ask me."

"What makes you say that?" O'Reilly said.

"She thinks she's something special because she married a man with money. She had nothing before she met Arnold."

"Why do you think she could be involved in his murder?" DC Owen said.

"Because she's a cold-hearted bitch. She comes in here like she owns the place, and she always gives the staff a hard time. Her and those kids need some lessons in manners."

"You know James and Vanessa too?" DC Owen said.

"Of course. James got one of the caddies fired a while ago."

"What happened?" O'Reilly said.

"James thought he could waltz onto the golf course, and be some kind of hotshot golfer, but he's far from it. He took a few lessons and lost the first game he played miserably. He blamed the caddy of course. Insisted that the club let him go. He's a nasty piece of work, and Vanessa isn't much better."

"We've yet to talk to her," O'Reilly said. "She's travelling around southeast Asia and we're having a hard time tracking her down."

Hillary frowned at him. The expression lasted quite some time and O'Reilly found it rather unsettling. "She's not in southeast Asia," Hillary said.

"We were led to believe she was," DC Owen said. "She finished her A Levels and went travelling with a few friends."

"I don't know who told you that, but I definitely saw her last night, walking away from the bar."

"You must be mistaken," O'Reilly said. "Everyone we've spoken to about her confirmed that Vanessa is thousands of miles away."

"Then she must have a doppelganger," Hillary said. "I know what I saw."

"What exactly did you see?" DC Owen said.

"Vanessa Green, plain as day."

"Where was this?" O'Reilly asked.

"At the Full Moon," Hillary said. "It's a club just down from Fort Hommet. I was there with a few friends last night, and I saw her. Vanessa Green is on the island."

CHAPTER THIRTY FIVE

The Full Moon was situated so close to the beach that the tables and chairs on the outside deck were covered in sand. There were no patrons sitting there and O'Reilly deduced the club was only open at night. From the deck the customers had a spectacular view across Vazon Bay. The fort stood proud to the north. A light westerly breeze was blowing in from the sea, and O'Reilly breathed it in.
"They say the air on the island is some of the cleanest in Europe," DC Owen informed him.
"You can taste it," O'Reilly said. "The air in Dublin always tasted of fish and rotten seaweed. I suppose you get used to it after a while."

A young man interrupted their discussion. O'Reilly didn't think he was out of his teens yet.

"We're closed."

"I gathered that," O'Reilly said. "Do you work here?"

The teenager nodded.

"Were you on duty last night?" O'Reilly asked him.

He received a laugh by way of a reply. "On duty?"

"Were you working here last night?" DC Owen said.

"I work here every weekend."

"I'll take that as a yes then," O'Reilly said.

He took out his ID.

The man took a step back. "Whoa. That had nothing to do with me. I wasn't even working in the VIP lounge when that happened."

"What on earth are you going on about?"

"The drugs."

"We're not here about drugs," O'Reilly said. "Do you have a name?"

"Michael."

That was all he offered, and O'Reilly realised that was all he was going to get.

"OK, Michael," he said. "We're not here about any drugs. We're interested in a young woman who might have been here last night. Her name is Vanessa Green."

"Never heard of her," Michael said.

DC Owen took out her phone. She'd found a photograph of Vanessa on Vazon High School's website, and she'd saved it to her phone.

She showed it to Michael. "This is Vanessa."

He looked at the screen for a long time.

"I can't say I recognise her."

"She attended Vazon High School," O'Reilly told him.

"Do I look like someone who could afford to go to Vazon High?"

"I have no idea. Are you sure you didn't see her last night."

"I don't think so."

"What time does the club open for business?" O'Reilly said.

"Seven," Michael said. "We're open from seven until two in the morning."

O'Reilly looked at his watch. It was just after two in the afternoon.

"What are you doing here now? If the club only opens at seven, why are you working now?"

Michael nodded to the sand covered tables and chairs. "I haven't been here very long, so I get all the shit jobs. I work from noon until three cleaning up the crap from the night before, then I work from seven until two in the morning. Look, I didn't see that girl last night, and I don't know who she is."

"Does the club have CCTV?" DC Owen asked.

"Of course," Michael said. "There are cameras everywhere inside, and a couple out here."

"Would you be able to retrieve the footage for us from last night?" O'Reilly said.

"Piece of cake. I'm not going to be working here forever you know. I'm off to university in the autumn. I'm doing Computer Science."

"Good for you," O'Reilly said. "Let's take a look at that footage, shall we?"

There were two other people inside the club. A man and a woman were cleaning tables and stocking up the bar at the back of the club. Neither of them acknowledged O'Reilly and DC Owen when they came in with Michael. O'Reilly looked around the interior of the Full Moon. The bar took up the entire back wall. A dancefloor stood in front of a metal balcony. The lights were on inside and the CCTV cameras were very obvious. O'Reilly counted eight of them in total. He wondered why they felt the need to have so many cameras.

He asked Michael as much.

"I haven't been here that long," the youngster reminded him. "But I heard it's something about covering their arses."

"I'm not following you," O'Reilly said.

"We've got four security staff here. Nightclub bouncers are notorious, aren't they? They get a bad rap for being a bit excessive at times, but that's not the case here. The owner installed the cameras so the customers can't make false claims against them. What is it you need to look at?"

"I want to know if Vanessa Green was here last night. We have a witness who claims she was, and I want to know for sure."

"Why are you so interested in this Green woman?" Michael asked. "What's she done?"

"That's not your concern. Could you show us the footage please."

He was surprised when Michael asked them to take a seat. He was expecting to be shown some kind of control room, but when the young man returned with a laptop, he realised technology was moving at a much faster pace than he could keep up with. Michael booted it up and set it down on the table.

"What time are we looking at?" he asked.

Hillary Green claimed she'd seen Vanessa Green just before midnight. O'Reilly asked Michael to run the footage from half an hour before that.

"She was seen leaving the bar," DC Owen remembered.

"We have two cameras pointing at the bar," Michael told her. "One on either side. I'll split the screen."

"It was busy last night," O'Reilly commented as he watched.

The bar was two-deep with people. There were four people working behind the counter. Michael was one of them.

He laughed. "This is nothing. You should see it when the season really gets going. We don't stop all night."

People came and went, and there was a lull in trade just before midnight.

"How do you keep up?" O'Reilly wondered.

"You get used to it," Michael said. "And there's a system in place. Two bar staff on either side. I was working on the left last night. We get to know what the regulars drink after a while and things go quicker. I don't see your mystery woman here."

"Keep watching."

DC Owen kept the photograph of Vanessa Green open on her phone the whole time. Michael glanced down at it every now and then.

"I think your witness must have made a mistake," he said as the time at the bottom of the screen told them it was almost twelve-thirty. "That girl wasn't here."

O'Reilly was starting to wonder the same thing. It was possible Hillary Green had mistaken someone else for Vanessa Green. The lighting in the club wasn't great, and it would be easy to make that mistake.

"There she is."

It was DC Owen who spotted her first. The clock on the screen read: 00:43.

"I didn't see her," O'Reilly said.

"Can you rewind it?" DC Owen asked Michael. "And play it in slow motion."

"No problem," he said.

He went back to 00:41 and started the tape at half speed. The woman DC Owen thought was Vanessa Green was nowhere to be seen.

"There," DC Owen said. "Pause it there."

"I still don't see her, Katie," O'Reilly said.

DC Owen pointed to the far right of the bar counter. A woman with long black hair was standing with her back to the cameras.

"You can't see her face," O'Reilly said.

"You will in a minute," DC Owen said. "She turns around just now."

Michael started the footage again. Forty-five seconds passed then the woman with the black hair turned around.

"You've got good eyes," Michael said to DC Owen. "I think you might be right. That's why I didn't remember her – she ordered her drink from the other side of the bar."

He restarted the footage, and they watched it frame by frame. He paused it when he believed the camera had captured the best angle, and he zoomed in slightly.

"I can't get too much of a close-up," he explained. "The image becomes pixelated, but this is quite a good shot."

O'Reilly's eyes alternated between DC Owen's phone and the image of the woman on the screen of the laptop. He did this a few times and nodded to himself.

"It's definitely her," he decided. "Vanessa Green isn't travelling around southeast Asia – she's right here on the island."

CHAPTER THIRTY SIX

"I can't believe we got away with using a dead man's credit card."

James Green was sitting up on the bed in the room on the third floor of the Guernsey Royal Hotel.

"How did you even get hold of it?" he added.

James was naked from the waist up. He was barefoot and the top button of the jeans he had on was unfastened.

"I've had it for a couple of years," Sasha Hillman said. "My dad linked a card up with his ages ago."

"They didn't even smell a rat when we checked in," James said.

"Why would they? There are plenty of rich kids on the island. A teenager with a credit card is hardly going to set off any alarms."

"Shall we order room service? We can put it on my dad's card this time."

Sasha laughed. "I think that would be asking for trouble. It'll all be added to the final bill. Let's get some lobster. I think good old John Hillman can afford it."

It was James's turn to laugh.

The sound of a mobile phone ringtone caused him to jump off the bed.

"Relax," Sasha said. "It's *my* phone."

She looked at the screen and rejected the call.

"Who was it?" James asked.

"Jeremy Hall."

"Urgh," James groaned. "He really has got it bad for you."

They called down for room service and a knock on the door thirty minutes later told them it had arrived. James put a T-Shirt on and went to answer it. A middle-aged woman came in with a trolley. She didn't utter a word to the two teenagers. She asked them if they required anything else - they told her they didn't, and she left them to it without even lingering for a tip.

"How long do you want to stay here?" James asked.

He picked up the lobster crackers and the seafood fork and examined them as though they were instruments of torture.

"As long as we feel like it," Sasha said.

"Do you even know how to use these things?" James held up the peculiar tools.

"I think you crack open the legs and the tail," Sasha said. "And get the meat out with the fork."

She watched as James attempted this. He made a real mess of it.

"Give them here," she said.

She did a much better job, and soon one of the lobsters had been well and truly dissected. She repeated the process with the other one.

They were halfway through the seafood feast when another phone rang. This time it was James's. He glanced at the screen and froze. The ringtone played on.

"Who is it?" Sasha asked in a voice no louder than a whisper.

James continued to stare at the screen.

"Who is it?" Sasha asked again.

James looked at her. "It's my sister."

* * *

"Vanessa Green has been seen on the island." O'Reilly and DC Owen had come straight back to the Island Police HQ after watching the CCTV footage from the Full Moon, and told everyone to stop what they were doing. He'd decided to discuss the significance of Vanessa's reappearance on the island.

"She was seen at a club by Fort Hommet," he said. "And when Katie and I checked the camera footage there, it was confirmed. We were led to believe that she was travelling around southeast Asia, so what is she doing back here?"

"It's possible she's heard about her father's murder," DCI Fish put forward. "She could have flown back because of that."

"If that's the case," O'Reilly said. "Why weren't we informed? Everybody we've spoken to claims they haven't been able to get hold of the girl, so how did she get word of her father's demise?"

"It's been all over the news, sir," DC Stone said. "Perhaps she was in contact with someone beside her family here. One of her friends could have let her know what was going on."

"You know what teenagers are like," DS Skinner said. "That kind of thing will have been all over social media."

"But she was thousands of miles away," O'Reilly argued.

"That means nothing these days," DC Owen said. "Girls of Vanessa's age check their social media accounts regularly. I think that's why she's back."

"It still doesn't explain why nobody has bothered to tell us about her return."

"Do we know who she was travelling with?" DC Owen asked.

"What difference does it make?" DC Stone said.

"It's just a thought I had. Find out who she was with over there and speak to their family. It's possible they'll know when Vanessa decided to come back."

"That's a great idea, Katie," O'Reilly said. "We'll be able to get the details of her travel plans via passport control, but you all know how long that will take."

"How do we even find out who she was on holiday with?" DCI Fish wondered.

"Social media," the DCs Owen and Stone said at the same time.

"I'm still not following you," DCI Fish said.

"If Vanessa Green hasn't posted anything about her travels in southeast Asia, sir," DC Owen said. "Then there's something seriously wrong with her. She's eighteen – there will be something on her Facebook, Twitter or Instagram about who she went away with."

CHAPTER THIRTY SEVEN

It didn't take long to find one of Vanessa Green's travelling companions. Like Vanessa, Serendipity Fraser had also been a student at Vazon High, and according to one of Vanessa's Facebook posts they'd arrived at Bangkok's Suvarnabhumi International Airport in Thailand on the 23rd of June. There was a third member of the party – a girl named Fiona Smith, but O'Reilly concluded that it would be much easier to find someone called Serendipity Fraser. It really was an unusual name. DC Owen found her in no time. She was listed on the school's class of 2019, and they soon had an address for her parents.

The Frasers had a huge apartment in a complex in Les Martins. It was an exclusive estate with only a few double-storey apartments. Situated a few hundred metres from the bay to the north, the views from the upper level were breathtaking. O'Reilly had phoned ahead, and Connor and Susan Fraser had been more than happy to talk to them.

Connor was a friendly man with bright blue eyes. He invited O'Reilly in and led them up a flight of stairs to the main living area. O'Reilly wasn't used to steps anymore and it took him quite a while.
"What happened to your leg?" Connor asked him. There was a hint of Scottish in his accent.

"Bike accident," O'Reilly told him.

"Motorbike?"

O'Reilly nodded. "I broke my femur."

"You were lucky. I've seen blokes end up with so many pins and plates in them they set off alarms when they walk through the metal detectors in the airport. Can I offer you something to drink? Coffee, tea or perhaps something a bit stronger."

"Tea would be grand," O'Reilly said.

"Make yourself comfortable over there," Connor pointed to a leather lounge suite. "I'll organise the drinks."

O'Reilly walked over to the huge window at the back of the room. The view from up here really was special. The apartment offered a panoramic view of the entire bay. The green of L'Ancresse Common could be seen to the east.

"This place is amazing," DC Owen said.

"The setup is a bit odd," O'Reilly said. "I wouldn't fancy climbing those stairs every day. It's strange that the bedrooms are all on the ground floor."

"A lot of places are like this now. They call it an upside-down design. I like it – it means the best views are from the main living areas."

Connor came back with a woman with short blond hair. He introduced her as Susan, his wife.

"Help yourself to the tea," she said.

O'Reilly did just that. "This is a very nice apartment."

"We love it," Susan said.

"How long have you been on the island?" O'Reilly asked.

"Just over five years," Connor said.

"That accent, it's Scottish, isn't it?"

"There's no fooling you. Edinburgh."

"What made you come to Guernsey?" DC Owen said.

"Politics," Connor replied.

"For a Scotsman," Susan explained. "My husband isn't the most patriotic of men."

"Nonsense," Connor argued. "I love Scotland as much as the next Jock. I made the decision to move when the talk of Scottish Independence got heated."

"You're against Scottish Independence?" O'Reilly said.

"It'll never work. The Scots are designed to be ruled by someone else. It's in our heritage. We may have a history of being fiercely proud of that heritage, but show me a Scotsman who professes to be able to govern Scotland and I'll show you a liar. I didn't want to be there when that kind of shit hit the fan."

"Language, Connor," Susan warned.

"Nonsense," he said, and turned to O'Reilly. "But you're not here to talk about the woes of Bonnie Scotland, are you?"

"No," O'Reilly said. "I believe your daughter is travelling around southeast Asia with Vanessa Green."

"Not anymore." It was Susan.

"I thought Serendipity, Vanessa and another girl set off together."

"Fiona Smith," DC Owen reminded him.

"Right," O'Reilly said. "Fiona Smith. Are they not travelling together?"

A loud noise could be heard downstairs. It sounded like church bells.

"We need to change that cursed doorbell chime," Connor said. "I can't stand the sound of church bells."

"I'll go and see who it is," Susan offered.

"Terrible business about what happened over on Rue La Mere," Connor said when she was gone.

"Did you know Arnold Green?" O'Reilly asked him. "And John Hillman. Your daughter attended the same school as James, Vanessa and Sasha, didn't she?"

"Aye," Connor said. "I met them a few times, but we didn't socialise. John seemed like a nice bloke, but I didn't like Arnold much."

"Why not?" DC Owen said.

"I'm generally a pretty decent judge of character. Take your man here – I could tell straight away he was one of the good ones."

"I'd reassess your belief in the accuracy of your judgement," O'Reilly said. "Not many people like me very much."

"Those ones are not worth knowing. You tell it like it is, and I like that."

Susan came back inside the room. "Sorry about that. It was an Amazon delivery."

"What have you ordered now, woman?" Connor asked. Susan winked at him. "That's none of your business."

"Before we were interrupted," O'Reilly said. "You said that Serendipity and Vanessa aren't travelling together. I don't understand."

"They flew out together," Connor explained. "But they parted ways as soon as they landed in Thailand. Serendipity told us in a Skype call."

"Did they have a falling out?" DC Owen said.

"Not really," Susan said. "It seems they had different agendas. Serendipity and Fiona thought it was going to be a trip of a lifetime. They wanted to do something different."

"They went there to see a bit of culture," Connor carried on. "But all Vanessa wanted to do was see the nightlife in the area. She stayed in Bangkok while the other two headed east to Vietnam."

"And that wasn't part of the plan?"

"We didn't think so," Susan said. "We've got nightclubs on the island. Why fly halfway around the world to do the same thing you do at home?"

"Do you know exactly when the girls parted ways?" O'Reilly said.

"They landed in Bangkok on the 23rd." Susan said. "I think it was a Sunday."

"The 23rd was a Sunday," DC Owen confirmed.

"And we spoke to Serendipity on the Monday," Connor said. "She and Fiona were already heading east to Vietnam, via Cambodia."

"But Vanessa remained in Bangkok?" O'Reilly said.

"That's right."

"Did they keep in contact? Do you know if Serendipity has heard from Vanessa since they parted ways."

"Not as far as I'm aware," Susan said.

"She hasn't mentioned it," Connor added.

"Can I ask why you're so interested in our daughter's trip abroad?" Susan said.

"We're just trying to get a better picture of what's happened in the last week or so," O'Reilly said.

"Nobody has heard from Vanessa Green since she left

for Thailand, and I'm trying to understand why that is."

"Do you think something has happened to her?" Connor asked.

"I don't know," O'Reilly admitted. "I really don't know."

CHAPTER THIRTY EIGHT

O'Reilly decided to chance his luck with Theresa Green again. He hoped she would have had a change of heart and would be willing to speak to him. He wanted to know if she was aware that her daughter was back on the island. If anyone knew that Vanessa was back in Guernsey, it would be her mother.

He was out of luck. After a two-minute one-way conversation O'Reilly admitted defeat and left her to the four walls of her holding cell. He told her that her silence was all very well, but it wasn't going to do her any favours if she wanted to be able go home anytime soon. She reacted with a shrug of the shoulders and that irritated the Irishman. He couldn't understand what she was planning, but he knew instinctively that she had something up her sleeve. Her indifference to her predicament was troubling him, and he couldn't fathom the significance of it.

He made some tea and leaned back in the chair in his office. It had been a strange day. The woman Arnold Green was having an affair with claimed to have seen Vanessa Green at a nightclub and the CCTV from the club had confirmed it. Why was she back on the island? She ought to be in southeast Asia right now, so what had brought her back to Guernsey? Perhaps he was looking in the wrong places for the answers he needed.

O'Reilly took out his phone and brought up DC Owen's number. He pressed call and waited.

"Sir," she answered it.

"Katie," O'Reilly said. "I want James Green and Sasha Hillman brought in."

"Do we know where they are?"

"I presume James is still staying at the school, and he ought to know where Sasha is. They seem to be close."

"I'll see what I can do," DC Owen said and rang off.

She called back five minutes later.

"We've got a problem, sir."

"I'm not a big fan of problems, Katie," O'Reilly told her. "What is it?"

"I called the school. It's Saturday, but the caretaker was there. He offered to check the accommodation, and it looks like James Green has gone."

"What do you mean, gone?" O'Reilly said.

"He's packed up his stuff and left. Nobody knows where he went."

"Damn it. What about the girl? What about Sasha Hillman?"

"I've asked uniform to go round to her house," DC Owen said. "It's possible she's there with James."

"Keep me informed."

"This just gets stranger and stranger," O'Reilly said to his teacup.

He was starting to wonder if he was caught up in some kind of complex screenplay. With a plot that was almost impossible to decipher, and characters that kept disappearing and appearing as the plot required, he wondered if everything that had happened on the island in the past few days had been carefully orchestrated. Three men were dead, and it was looking more and more as though there were a whole host of players involved. Was the confusion they'd created intentional? Was it designed to send the Island Police round and round in circles? If that was the case, O'Reilly had to admit that they'd succeeded. He had no idea where to look next.

Help arrived from an unexpected quarter. When O'Reilly's phone rang he thought it must be one of the uniforms sent out to see if Sasha Hillman had gone back to Rue La Mere.

It wasn't, and when O'Reilly realised who it was, he almost hung up.

"O'Reilly," he answered the call.

"I have some information for you."

It was Fred Viking.

"Tell someone who cares, Viking," O'Reilly said.

"That's no way to talk to someone who might have some useful info."

"Wasting police time is a criminal offence."

"Aren't you even curious?" Fred asked.

"I haven't got time for games," O'Reilly said. "What do you want?"

"I told you. I have something you might find very interesting, but I want something in return."

O'Reilly expected as much.

"Talk," he said. "And make it quick."

"Not on the phone," Fred said. "Meet me at the Herald's offices, and we can talk there. How does five suit you?"

"Fine," O'Reilly found himself saying.

"You won't be disappointed."

The silence on the other end of the line told O'Reilly that he'd hung up.

He realised that Fred the Ed hadn't mentioned what this information was going to cost him, and this piqued his curiosity. He decided that it wouldn't hurt to see what the repugnant editor had to tell him. What harm could it do?

When the phone started to ring again O'Reilly wondered if Fred Viking had called back to tell him what he wanted from the quid pro quo deal. It wasn't the editor of the Island Herald – it was PC Greg Hill.

"Sasha Hillman isn't at number 4 Rue La Mere, sir," he said.

"Are you absolutely sure?" O'Reilly asked.

"Positive, sir. There's nobody there. The house is empty. And the neighbour said she hasn't seen anyone coming and going."

"What neighbour?" O'Reilly said.

"Jane Dodds. The wife of the third victim. She's still in a bit of a state, but she told us she's been sitting in a chair staring out of the front window for hours. If someone had gone next door, she would have noticed it. She spotted me and Kim straight away."

"Thanks for letting me know," O'Reilly said.

He was at a loss for what to do now. The only positive lead they had was a tip off from the unscrupulous editor of the local rag, and it didn't exactly fill him with confidence. The clock on the wall told him it was just after four, so he decided to take a slow walk to the offices of the Island Herald.

CHAPTER THIRTY NINE

As he walked O'Reilly compiled a list of possible suspects in his head. The play that was being acted out on the island had quite a cast, and O'Reilly imagined them as their names would appear on the cast list. Who were the main players in this drama? And how was this story going to end? He was damned if he was just going to sit back and let the director of the action have it his own way. He was adamant that he was going to change the narrative so that this play had a happy ending. The bad guys were going to come out second best if O'Reilly had anything to do with it.

He carried on west on La Grange and turned left onto Victoria Road. An aroma caught his attention as he passed a row of shops. It was coming from the bakery. It was irresistible and O'Reilly found himself inside the shop without even realising it. His legs had taken him there without his permission.

He selected a meat pie from behind a glass counter, paid for it and went back outside into the sunshine. He sat on a bench in front of the St Joseph and St Mary Catholic Church. He closed his eyes, took in the scent of the pie then tucked in. It was devoured in two minutes flat.

The gate that led to the church grounds was open and O'Reilly decided to take a look inside. He still had plenty of time before his appointment with Fred Viking, and it had been a very long time since he'd set foot inside a church. He stopped for a moment to take in the building. The old church looked like it had been well maintained over the years. The brickwork was sound, and the turquoise spire shone brightly in the afternoon sun. A weather cock faced north at its tip.

O'Reilly stepped inside the church and breathed in deeply. Churches had a unique smell to them. It didn't matter where the church was, they always smelled the same - there was always the musty tang of old wood and ancient prayerbooks. He took a pew at the front and gazed up at the stained-glass window behind the pulpit. Joseph and Mary stood guard on either side.

"It's been a while," O'Reilly said.
He'd never been particularly religious. His mother and father had allowed him to choose, and he'd opted to play it by ear. There had been a time when his wife was nearing the end when O'Reilly had spoken to God

quite a lot, but then Mary died, and the conversations with the man upstairs died too. O'Reilly became disillusioned with religion, and he'd turned his back on it.

But now he was back in a church talking to a God he didn't really believe in, and he wasn't sure what had brought him here.

"It just seemed like the right thing to do," he spoke to the stained-glass window. "I'm not here to ask any favours of you – that would be presumptuous of me, but it doesn't hurt to stay acquainted, does it?"

Somebody coughed behind him, and O'Reilly turned around. A man in a white T-shirt was standing at the back of the church taking an interest in the Irishman at the front. He walked over and O'Reilly stood up.

"I was just about to be on my way."

"Is there something on your mind?" the man asked. He introduced himself as Oscar Davies.

"Or Father Davies if you like," he added.

O'Reilly shook his hand.

"You don't look like any of the Fathers I remember when I was a kid."

"Times have changed. Did you get what you came for?"

"I don't really know what I came for," O'Reilly told him.

"I think you do. Our doors are always open."

"That's good to know. I'd better be off. This is a really nice church you've got here. It really is."

He went back outside and turned onto Victoria Road again. He stared at the road sign and goosebumps started to form on his arms. The prickling crept up to his shoulders and spread to his neck. *Victoria*, he thought.

That's what had prompted him to step foot inside a church for the first time in ages. He'd been here before, and he was determined to make sure that this time things would be different. It didn't hurt to have a bit of help, even if he didn't really believe in the big man. It didn't hurt to hedge your bets.

He was taken back to a few years ago. It was six months after Mary's diagnosis. It pained him to see that she was by far the stronger of the two of them. That should have been his responsibility but, more often than not it was his wife who had comforted him and not the other way round. He'd regretted that ever since, and he was determined not to let it happen again should it come to that with Victoria.

Mary had had good days close to the end. There were times when the old Mary would resurface and O'Reilly would make the mistake of embracing it to such an extent that everything he had inside him would drain out when she lapsed again. It had almost finished him at one stage.

Two weeks before the cancer took her away forever O'Reilly had even been led to believe that she'd beaten it. He'd just finished a tiring night shift, and he'd come home to a full Irish breakfast. He'd walked inside the kitchen to find Mary pottering around in the kitchen like she used to. She made him sit down and eat, and afterwards they'd talked for longer than they had in years. It was like the old days just after Assumpta was born. In the rare hours when she'd given them a few hours rest O'Reilly and Mary had sat together and just talked. They'd made plans, and O'Reilly was sure those plans would be realised someday.

Neither of them had banked on Mary's illness scuppering those plans. They hadn't bargained on that at all. The cancer had arrived without warning and by the time it had made its presence known it was too late. Mary died two weeks after making O'Reilly the best breakfast he'd ever had. He didn't eat another full Irish breakfast for a very long time afterwards.

"Are you alright?"

O'Reilly realised Father Davies was standing in front of him.

"I was miles away there," he said.

"God is always here for you," Father Davies said. "He's always willing to listen."

"I'll bear that in mind," O'Reilly told him. "I'll bear that in mind."

CHAPTER FORTY

Fred Viking was there in person to meet O'Reilly when he went inside the building that housed the offices of the island's biggest newspaper. The editor of the Island Herald was standing by the reception desk, and he appeared to be alone there.

"It's good to see you," he said and extended his hand.

O'Reilly decided to offer him a bit of charity and shook the hand.

"We share a history, O'Reilly," Fred said. "We haven't known each other long and yet we've managed to cross paths often."

"What do you want to tell me?" O'Reilly asked.

"All in good time. First we need to discuss the nitty gritty."

"What is it you want from me?"

"I want the Herald to be the first to know the inside

info."

"You know I can't promise you that," O'Reilly said. "I knew this would be a waste of time."

He turned to leave but Fred stopped him with a hand on his shoulder.

"Take your hand off me now," O'Reilly said.

Fred did as he was asked. "Calm down. This is going to be worth your while."

"I cannot discuss details of an ongoing investigation with the press," O'Reilly said. "You know that."

"I'm not asking for full disclosure, Liam."

O'Reilly winced. It was the first time Fred Viking had used his first name.

"What are you asking for?"

"A head's-up now and again," Fred said. "Something to put me ahead of the competition."

"The competition happens to be my daughter," O'Reilly reminded him. "You seem to be forgetting that."

"And I know for a fact the same rules don't apply there."

"Can we just get down to business?" O'Reilly said. "It's been a long day, and this is the last thing I need."

"You'll like what I have to say."

"Spit it out then."

"Follow me," Fred said. "You won't regret this. I've got a feeling our relationship is about to move to another level after this."

"Why does that make me feel slightly ill?" O'Reilly asked.

Fred ignored the comment. "Come on."

They went inside his office, and he asked O'Reilly to take a seat. He walked over to a filing cabinet and unlocked the top drawer. He took out a file and placed it on the desk in front of O'Reilly.

"What's this?" the Irish detective pointed at it.

"We still haven't discussed my request."

"I am not feeding you information."

"How about a compromise," Fred suggested.

"What kind of compromise?"

"I'm taking a big chance here. But I'm in a good mood and I'm going to give you the benefit of the doubt. If you decide that what is contained within that file is worth something, you give me what you believe it's worth. It's not an unreasonable trade."

It wasn't, and O'Reilly found himself agreeing.

"What exactly is in there?" he asked.

Fred pulled it towards him and opened it. He leafed through a few pieces of paper, found the one he was looking for and handed it to O'Reilly.

"What is this?" O'Reilly said.

"Something that could cause a lot of trouble for the person I got it from if it came out that he gave it to me."

O'Reilly looked closely at what was on the sheet of paper.

"It looks like some kind of building plans."

"That's because it is," Fred confirmed. "These are the architectural plans for a development on the island. The plans are yet to be approved, but they will be, if you know what I mean."

"What exactly are they planning on building?" O'Reilly said.

He was no architect and the design in front of him didn't look like any building he'd seen before.

"This is an ultra-modern hotel. It is a hotel like no other on the island, and the architect who designed it has even claimed it is one that will rival any luxury hotel anywhere in the world."

O'Reilly looked more carefully at the plans.

"How did you even get hold of this? Surely if this thing is as special as you've made it out to be the designer wouldn't just hand out the plans to anyone."

"A peculiar series of events led to me getting my hands on it," Fred said. "I won't bore you with the details. We'd be here all day. What you are privy to right now is indeed top secret."

"And yet I'm looking at it right now."

"The architect responsible is no longer working for the company he worked for when he designed the hotel," Fred told him. "They had a falling out about some of the specifics."

"And they let him keep the plans?"

"Of course not, but it was all imprinted on his brain, and it was simple to recreate it. I'm sure you appreciate what would happen if his identity were revealed. He signed an NDA, and this is a blatant contravention of that NDA. That's a non-disclosure-agreement in case you weren't aware."

"I know what an NDA is," O'Reilly said. "So, a new hotel is going to be built on the island. How is that relevant to my investigation?"

Fred took out another sheet of paper from the file. "This is an arial prediction of what the hotel will look like when it's completed."

O'Reilly tapped his finger on the paper. "I assume this is the sea."

"That's Vazon Bay," Fred said. "A little way back is the main Vazon beach road and behind that is a few hectares of open ground. It's protected land which means it isn't zoned for habitation."

"Nobody can build on it," O'Reilly said.

"Correct. Which means the proposed hotel will have unobstructed views across the bay. The developers will never have to worry about that view being taken away, and that makes the land behind it extremely valuable."

"My geography of the island is still a little bit sketchy," O'Reilly admitted. "Where exactly is this hotel going to be built?"

"You know it well," Fred told him.

A mobile phone started to ring somewhere inside the office. Fred made no effort to answer it.

"I think I'm starting to get an idea what you're getting at," O'Reilly said.

"This is Rue La Mere, isn't it?"

"Death Rue," Fred said. "I was rather pleased with that one."

"Those houses are on the site of the proposed development of the hotel," O'Reilly said.

"You've got it in one," Fred said. "The most luxurious hotel this island has ever seen is going to be built where numbers 2, 4 and 6 Rue La Mere are currently situated."

CHAPTER FORTY ONE

"Have I got your attention?" Fred Viking asked. O'Reilly had fallen silent when he realised the implications of what the editor of the Island Herald had just told him.

"How many other people know about this?" O'Reilly said.

"The architect of course. The construction firm due to carry out the building work, and the investors. And now me and you. It's significant, isn't it?"

It was, but O'Reilly knew better than to admit it to a hack like Fred Viking.

"A major company is planning on building a state-of-the-art hotel on the site where three men have been murdered," Fred said.

"Benjamin Dodds wasn't murdered at home," O'Reilly said without thinking.

"Go on," Fred said.

"I've said enough."

"Come on, O'Reilly. I've given you this on a plate. This is big, and you know it. Tell me what you're allowed to tell me."

O'Reilly did. He gave him the bare minimum, but the expression on Fred Viking's face announced that it was enough.

"How much is this thing going to cost?" he asked afterwards. "How much is this hotel going to set back the investors?"

"That's not important," Fred said. "I have it on good authority that they already have a buyer lined up. A French billionaire is said to have shown a very real interest in the project."

"I'm not following you."

"The development is not going to happen overnight," Fred said. "And the initial cost will be through the roof, what with the acquisition of the land and the building materials, but the end product will be worth it. Rumour has it that when the hotel is finished the figure is somewhere close to half a billion. Five-hundred-million pounds."

"Sweet Jesus." O'Reilly couldn't help himself.

"There are going to be some disgustingly rich people by the end of this."

"I don't suppose you happen to know who these investors are," O'Reilly said.

Fred raised an eyebrow. "Come on, O'Reilly. Do you want me to do all of the hard work for you? That's about all I can tell you. The question now is what's it worth to you?"

O'Reilly didn't have an answer to this. He had to admit that if what Fred Viking had told him was true it put a whole new perspective on the investigation. This was much bigger than he thought. It wasn't a simple case of murder for money - this was a monster of gigantic proportions and O'Reilly wasn't quite sure if his team were equipped to deal with something like it.

"Well?" Fred said. "I've given you something, what do I get in return?"

"Let me sleep on it," O'Reilly said.

With that he got to his feet.

"Are you taking the piss?" Fred said and also stood up.

"Look, Viking," O'Reilly said. "I appreciate what you've told me, but I need to do some more digging before I decide what to do with the info."

"I had you pegged as a man of your word."

"I am a man of my word," O'Reilly said. "I'll see what I can do. I can't promise any more than that. You might want to warn your architect friend though."

"Warn him about what?"

"If what we both suspect turns out to be well-founded, it means we're dealing with some very dangerous people. Your man needs to make himself scarce. He needs to hide, and he needs to stay hidden. I'll be in touch."

This time it was O'Reilly who offered his hand. Fred didn't hesitate before shaking it.

"Thank you," O'Reilly managed. "I really do appreciate it."

"Can I quote you on that?" Fred said.

"If you do, I'll deny it. Like I said, I'll be in touch."

Later O'Reilly would admit to having no recollection of the walk to his apartment on Belmont Road. When he walked through the entrance of the Mt Herman complex, he realised he'd walked the whole way on autopilot. He had a lot on his mind and the five-hundred metres he'd travelled had passed by in a blur.

The conversation with Fred Viking had been a truly surreal one. O'Reilly and Fred the Ed had clashed heads almost as soon as the Irishman had stepped foot on the island, and they'd despised one another ever since, but the atmosphere in the office of the editor of the Herald had been almost convivial. And the information he'd passed on could be the key to the entire investigation. For the first time since the start of the case they had a very promising motive. Everything Fred had told him tied in with what had happened on the island in the past few days.

O'Reilly went inside his apartment and was met by Bram and Juliet.

"Hello, hooligans. How was your day? Mine was fekkin bizarre."

The cats weren't interested in O'Reilly's day. They wanted food and they wanted it now. He filled up their bowls and took a beer out of the fridge. He took it outside and sat down in the small patio area. His phone started to ring in his pocket. The screen told him it was someone he hadn't spoken to in months.

"Darren," he answered it. "I've been meaning to talk to you."

Darren Jenkins was his landlord. He was a strange man in his early thirties. When O'Reilly had first been introduced to him, he got the impression he was scared of the Irishman.

"Mr O'Reilly," Darren said.

"You can call me Liam," O'Reilly said. "I told you that."

"What is it you wanted to talk to me about?"

"You phoned me remember."

"Ah, right. This is rather delicate."

"Delicate?" O'Reilly repeated.

"I don't know whether you're aware," Darren said.

"That I own three apartments in the Mt Herman complex."

"I wasn't."

"I'm afraid I've had a complaint from Mr France next door."

"Go on."

"Mr France has alleged you threatened him."

"I assure you I did not," O'Reilly said.

"Oh. Mr France claims you did."

"What exactly did he tell you?"

"He said your cats have been fighting with his cat," Darren said. "And when he asked you to do something about it, you became aggressive."

"They're cats, man," O'Reilly said. "They're wild beasts. Cats fight – end of story. What do you want me to do about it?"

"Get them to stop."

"They're cats," O'Reilly said. "Cats do not take orders from anyone. The neighbour is overreacting."

"He's lodged an official complaint. And as such I can't ignore it."

"What exactly does that mean?" O'Reilly asked.

"I'm afraid that if it happens again, action may be taken."

"Action? What the devil are you talking about? The man is an idiot. He's got nothing better to do than whine about inane things. Will there be anything else? I haven't got time for this."

"I'm just giving you a friendly warning, Mr O'Reilly."

"And you can stick your friendly warning up your fekkin arse, you gutless wonder."

The line went quiet for a while and O'Reilly wondered if his landlord had hung up on him.

He hadn't.

"I'm afraid you leave me no choice," Darren said and took a very loud deep breath. "I'm obliged to give you the mandatory three months' notice but after that you'll have to vacate the property."

O'Reilly did some quick mental arithmetic. That meant he had to be out by the end of September. It was perfect timing. He would be moving in with Victoria then anyway. The timing couldn't have been any more perfect.

"No problem," O'Reilly said. "No problem at all."

He was the one to hang up first.

CHAPTER FORTY TWO

After getting another beer O'Reilly thought about what he was going to do. He knew he needed to tell someone about the conversation at the Island Herald, but first he needed to process what the information Fred Viking had given him meant. A hotel was going to be built on the site where two men had been murdered in the past week. Another man who lived on the street had also been killed. O'Reilly didn't know much about property acquisition and construction, but he guessed there was a lot of red tape to overcome before such a massive project could get off the ground. There was planning permission to consider, and he wondered how long this particular project had been in the pipeline.

In the end he decided to give Tom Fish a call. DCI Fish wasn't as experienced as O'Reilly where murder was concerned, but he had been on the island a very long time and he would probably know more about the ins and outs of property law than anyone else on the team.

DCI Fish answered straight away.
"Tom," O'Reilly said. "I'm not disturbing you, am I?"
"I've only just walked through the door," DCI Fish said. "Anne's fast asleep."
"Leave her be," O'Reilly advised. "Enjoy the peace. I need to pick your brain."
"Go ahead."

O'Reilly outlined what Fred Viking had told him. He made sure he told DCI Fish everything.
"How reliable is this information?" the DCI asked when he was finished.

"It sounded legit," O'Reilly said. "And it makes sense. If it is true, we've really underestimated what we're dealing with. We've been fishing for small fry, when we should have been going for the sharks."

"I have no idea what you just said."

"This is much bigger than we thought," O'Reilly translated. "We're talking about a massive operation here. I'm starting to think this was never about three individual men. They were a small part of it, but there's a plan in place that is infinitely more complicated than we'd considered. And for that plan to succeed there needs to be a whole cast of players involved. I've never said this before, but I don't think we're going to win this one."

"There's always a way, Liam," DCI Fish said.

"What do you suggest we do? I have no idea how to proceed. I think we're way out of our depth."

"Leave it with me. I think I just heard Anne stir. Leave it with me and I'll see what I can do. We will get to the heart of this."

"How difficult is it to get a project like this off the ground?" O'Reilly asked.

"There are a lot of obstacles to overcome," DCI Fish said. "First you have to get approval to demolish the existing buildings, and then you need planning permission to be able to erect the new buildings."

"I thought it was simply a case of knocking down one place and building another."

"When the plans for the new structure are submitted, there are a lot of things to take into account. The new building might need more electrical connections for example, and then there's the aesthetic aspect to consider. You can't just put up any old eyesore on the island – it has to conform to the standards set out in law."

"So, it's a time-consuming process," O'Reilly said.

"It certainly is. Like I said, let me give it some thought, and we'll discuss it in more detail in the morning. I'll speak to an old school friend of mine. He invests in property, and he keeps his ear to the ground. He might have heard a rumour about the new hotel."

"I've got a terrible feeling about this, Tom."

"We'll figure it out. When have we ever failed to figure it out?"

O'Reilly hoped so. He'd been involved in some high-profile investigations in Ireland, but he'd never come across anything as complicated as this. Fred Viking had said there was half a billion pounds involved. O'Reilly wasn't even sure he knew how to write that figure down. It really was an astronomical amount of money.

The cats came outside and headed straight for the gap in the bushes between O'Reilly's apartment and the one next door.

"You have my blessing to do whatever you want," O'Reilly shouted after them. "Give little Timothy a good walloping from me."

He smiled, but it didn't last. The sound of his ringtone wiped it clean off his face.

It was DC Owen.

"Katie," O'Reilly answered it.

"Sorry to bother you, sir," she said. "But we've found something interesting."

"Are you still at work?"

"Of course. It's not yet six."

"What have you got?"

"Andy thought it might be a good idea to take a look through the bank statements we managed to get hold of. From all three victims. He noticed something strange when he went through John Hillman's. There were a few transactions on there that didn't make sense. According to the statement, last week John used his credit card to fill up with petrol in Castel, but five minutes later the card was used at a McDonalds here in St Peter Port. There is no way he would be able to get here from Castel in five minutes."

"How exactly does that help us?" O'Reilly said.

"Andy wondered if it could be fraud, so he called the call centre. It took a bit of persuading, but after explaining who he was he managed to get some information. Sasha Hillman has a credit card that's linked to her father's."

"Interesting."

"That's not all, sir. That credit card was used recently."

"As in after John was murdered?"

"It was used less than an hour ago," DC Owen said. "At the Guernsey Royal Hotel here in St Peter Port. It looks like Sasha Hillman is here in the capital."

CHAPTER FORTY THREE

O'Reilly asked DC Owen to pick him up from his apartment. He had no idea where the Guernsey Royal Hotel was, and he reckoned he'd done enough walking for one day. He needed to give his tired legs a rest. As it turned out the high-end hotel was less than a kilometre from his apartment. The missing schoolgirl had been ten minutes away from where he lived the whole time.

He brought DC Owen up to date with the developments pertaining to the planned hotel during the drive and she filled him in on what he'd missed back at the station.

"I still can't see how two teenagers can possibly be involved in this," she said. "This is serious stuff. It's not something two schoolkids could come up with."

"I don't believe they're the ones who orchestrated the plan," O'Reilly said. "But they are involved somehow, even if their roles have been minor ones."

"Five-hundred-million pounds is a hefty price to pay for a hotel, isn't it?"

"It certainly is," O'Reilly agreed. "But from what I've been told, this isn't any old hotel. Not only is it supposed to be one of the most luxurious hotels in the world, it's being built on prime island land. Half a billion pounds sounds surreal. I don't even know how many noughts there are in half a billion."

"Eight," DC Owen educated him. "Did you know there are more than two thousand billionaires in the world now? It's crazy to think about all that money?"

"I remember when a person that way inclined aspired to be a millionaire," O'Reilly said. "Now every Tom, Dick and Harry has a million quid."

He wasn't expecting the scene that was waiting for him at the Guernsey Royal Hotel. Three police cars were parked in the street opposite the main entrance. DC Stone's car was also there, as was DS Skinner's.

"This is a bit excessive, isn't it?" he said to DC Owen. "Who authorised it?"

"It was the DS," she said.

"They're two schoolkids, Katie," O'Reilly said. "It's not like we're dealing with Bonnie and Clyde."

"You know how DS Skinner is. You weren't around and neither was the DCI, so the DS made the call."

"I suppose he does tend to err on the side of caution. Let's hope all of this proves to be unnecessary."

DC Owen parked behind one of the police cars. O'Reilly got out and his phone started to ring. The screen told him it was an unknown number, so he let it go to voicemail. He spotted DS Skinner and DC Stone and walked over to them.

"The reinforcements are a bit over the top, Will."

"It is a bit of overkill," DS Skinner agreed. "But I didn't want to take any chances."

"Do we know if James Green is in there with Sasha?" O'Reilly asked.

"According to the receptionist, Sasha Hillman checked in earlier today. She was with a boy around her age, but we've yet to confirm if it's James or not. How do you want to play it?"

"We don't go in guns blazing," O'Reilly said. "That's for sure. How about a couple of officers knock on the door of the hotel room and ask them to come with them?"

"Sound like a good plan, sir."

"There's no time like the present. Come on then."

"You and me?" DS Skinner said.

"Why not? What room are they in?"

"612. It's on the sixth floor."

"We're definitely taking the lift then."

O'Reilly and DS Skinner stepped out of the elevator into the spacious lobby of the sixth floor of the Royal Guernsey Hotel. O'Reilly's phone started to ring again. This time he didn't even bother to see who was calling him.

"Do you want to do the honours, Will," he said.

DS Skinner knocked hard on the door.

"Did you hear that?" he said. "There's someone in there."

O'Reilly put his ear to the door. DS Skinner was right – he could hear the sound of someone moving behind the door.

"Sasha Hillman," he shouted. "Open the door. Police."

The door remained closed.

O'Reilly's ringtone started up again.

"Damn that thing," he said. "Why can't people just leave me alone?"

He banged on the door. "Sasha. Open up – we know you're in there."

"Leave us alone," a muffled voice said.

It was a male voice.

"James," O'Reilly said. "Is that you? You need to open the door and come with us. There's nowhere for you to go."

"Go away."

This voice was definitely female.

"Go and see if you can find some kind of master key," O'Reilly said.

"No problem, sir," DS Skinner said.

"And it might be an idea to bring a couple of uniforms back with you. These rich kids are really starting to annoy me. I don't know whether they're going to come quietly or not, and I don't want to take any chances. PC Woodbine ought to scare them into submission."

The doors had barely closed on the elevator DS Skinner was in when there was a quiet click and the door to the hotel room was opened an inch. O'Reilly took a step back. This wasn't part of the plan.

"You're completely surrounded," he said and realised how ridiculous he sounded.

Sasha and James were a pair of schoolkids.

"You need to come out," O'Reilly added. "And don't do anything you might live to regret."

He opened the door wider and peered inside. James Green and Sasha Hillman were sitting on the bed. Both of them were smiling at the Irishman in the doorway. O'Reilly opened his mouth to say something but stopped when he realised there was someone else inside the room. On the chair next to the bed was a third person. O'Reilly had never met her before, but he'd seen photographs. Vanessa Green had been found.

The door banged open, and PC Woodbine and PC Hill rushed in.

"I don't think they're going to give you any trouble," O'Reilly said. "I'll leave you to it."

He left the room and his phone started to ring again. This time he answered it. He didn't have the number saved on his phone, but he recognised the voice after just five words.

"Where the hell are you?"

It was Tommy Radcliffe, Victoria's brother.

O'Reilly walked down the corridor towards the elevator, holding the phone to his ear the whole time.

He emerged from the lift on the ground floor, DC Owen took one look at his face and raced over to him. "What's happened, sir?"

O'Reilly looked her in the eyes and frowned. "Katie?"

"Sir? What's wrong?"

"Victoria," he said. "She's been rushed to hospital. She's unconscious, and they can't seem to be able to wake her up."

CHAPTER FORTY FOUR

DCI Fish had known Hugh Lincoln for most of his life. The two friends had grown up on the same street, they'd attended the same school and sixth form college, and they'd even considered studying at the same university in England. That was when they'd decided to go their separate ways. DCI Fish had completed a law degree at Durham University while Hugh had studied Business in Paris.

Hugh had come back to the island and started his own investment company. It had been a very lucrative move, and he'd made a lot of money in a short space of time. He was a shrewd operator, and he kept a keen eye on the markets. And that was why DCI Fish had decided to drive over to Richmond now. He knew that if anyone on the island had heard a rumour about the new hotel in Vazon it would be Hugh.

He wasn't disappointed.

"How did you hear about this?" Hugh asked.

He poured a couple of whiskeys into glasses and handed one to DCI Fish.

DCI took a small sip and winced. "It's come to our attention during the course of an investigation. What can you tell me about it?"

Hugh downed his glass and poured another. "It's not yet set in stone, but I've heard something about a French buyer."

"Do you know who's behind it?"

"Behind the development?" Hugh said. "That I don't know. How is it you know about this? You seem to know more than I do."

"I'm afraid I can't tell you that."

"Is this connected to the recent murders in Vazon?"

DCI Fish knew better than to lie about this. It was quite obvious that it was connected.

He answered in the affirmative.

"Is there any way you can do some digging around?" he added.

"I'll see what I can do," Hugh replied. "This sounds serious."

"It is. And I've got a feeling we're way out of our depth. Nothing like this has ever happened on the island before. It's like something out of a film. What else can you tell me about this hotel?"

"I heard about it about a year ago, but I wasn't sure if it would ever go ahead."

"Why is that?"

"Because of the very nature of property investment," Hugh said. "I'm not one to blow my own trumpet, but I haven't done so well without making absolutely sure the investments I put my faith in are sound. And risk assessment is a major part of that. As far as I'm aware this hotel project is extremely risky. There are far too many variables in place, and I wouldn't touch a project like that with a bargepole."

"Are you saying that there are too many things to go wrong with it?" DCI Fish said.

"Definitely. You must be familiar with the term getting one's ducks in a row?"

"Of course."

"Well in this case, that row of ducks would reach to

the moon and back. First, the existing properties on the proposed site need to be acquired, and that's tricky when individual homeowners are concerned. Then you've got the planning permission involved. There are ways around that of course, but it's always a headache. There's the nightmare of the local outrage when a massive operation like this starts up. There will always be protests when a huge building like this is in its early stages. Like I say, I wouldn't touch a project like this for all the money in the world."

"Not even for half a billion?" DCI Fish said.

"The rewards don't warrant the risks."

"Unless you eliminate those risks."

Hugh finished his second glass of whiskey and stared at his friend.

"You shouldn't really be having this conversation with me, should you?"

"I know it won't go any further," DCI Fish said.

"That goes without saying. How's Anne? It's not long now, is it?"

"A couple of weeks. We both can't wait for the baby to pop out. What about you? Are there any babies in the pipeline for you and Jackie?"

"I don't think babies feature in our future. Both of us are too busy to take on that kind of responsibility." Hugh's wife, Jackie worked for an investment banking firm in Paris.

"I'd better get going," DCI Fish said. "Thank you for the advice."

"I hope it was useful," Hugh said.

"I believe it was."

"I'll do some more digging. Make some phone calls."

"I'd appreciate it," DCI Fish said. "We must make plans to grab a bite to eat some time. After the madness of the baby dies down a bit."

"Definitely," Hugh got to his feet and shook DCI Fish's hand. "I'll see what else I can find out for you."

DCI Fish opened the door to his car and got inside. He closed the door and sat there without starting the engine. He pondered over what his old friend had told him. The investigation had taken a rather sinister turn. This wasn't a simple case of a killing for financial gain – this was on another level altogether. Three men had lost their lives and there were more people involved that anyone on the team had ever come across before. This was evil on a grand scale.

DCI Fish turned the key in the ignition and reversed out of the driveway. He turned right onto Les

Banques and headed south back to St Peter Port. The lights on Herm were glowing to his left. The moon was full and a few sailboats were enjoying the balmy evening in the bay. Soon it would be July and Guernsey would spring to life. It was DCI Fish's favourite time on the island, and it was a time he always looked forward to.

But now something rotten had crawled inside the woodwork of the island he was born on. Something evil was eating its way through the heart of DCI Fish's home, and he wasn't sure how to stop it. It was a cancer, and it was spreading quickly. There was evil on the island, and even though DCI Fish knew it was there, he didn't have a clue where to look for it.

CHAPTER FORTY FIVE

"Why didn't you answer your damn phone?"
Tommy Radcliffe was standing opposite O'Reilly in the waiting room at the Princess Elizabeth Hospital. O'Reilly had just arrived. Victoria had been in ICU since she was rushed to the hospital in St Peter Port – she still hadn't regained consciousness, and the doctors weren't sure why this was.

"I'm sorry," O'Reilly said. "I was busy apprehending a couple of suspects."
"You should have answered your phone," Tommy said.
"I'm here now. What happened?"
"Nobody knows. Vic replaced the battery on the bike

and took it out for a spin. A motorist found her up in Les Martins and called an ambulance."

"Was she injured?" O'Reilly asked. "Is she here because of the accident or is it something to do with the cancer?"

"I don't know, Liam. Nobody seems to know what the hell is going on."

O'Reilly sat down and rubbed his eyes. He wasn't expecting this, and he didn't know what to do. A woman in a white coat came in and walked over to Tommy. She introduced herself as Dr Knight.

"She's woken up."

"Is she going to be alright?" O'Reilly asked.

"This is Liam," Tommy said. "Victoria's fiancé."

"She was lucky," Dr Knight said. "Apparently she wasn't travelling very fast when she lost consciousness."

"She passed out on the bike?" O'Reilly said.

"It appears that's what happened. She's sustained a few cuts and bruises, but the helmet she was wearing prevented anything more serious from happening."

"Why did she pass out?" O'Reilly said.

"She said she was feeling a bit lightheaded earlier in the shop," Tommy said. "I offered to drive her home, but you know what Vic's like."

O'Reilly did. She was more stubborn than he was.

"Can we go in and see her?" he asked Dr Knight.

"Make it quick," she said. "She needs to rest. We're going to keep her in for a while, and we need to do some tests to find out why she lost consciousness."

"Has it got something to do with the cancer?" O'Reilly said.

"It's highly unlikely. We'll do some tests, but it was probably due to the side-effects of the radiation treatment. She shouldn't really have been out on the motorbike."

"I'll make sure she doesn't do it again. I'll just pop my head in and say hello."

"Five minutes," Dr Knight said.

"Five minutes," O'Reilly repeated.

Victoria had been transferred to a private room. She was sitting up in the bed when O'Reilly and Tommy went inside.

O'Reilly took her hand and squeezed it. It was very warm.

"How are you feeling?"

"Embarrassed," she croaked.

"Don't be," O'Reilly said. "It happens to the best of us."

"Where's your stick?"

"In the cupboard at home where it belongs. I don't need it anymore."

Victoria looked up at her brother. "I hope you two have been getting along."

Tommy shrugged his shoulders. "What happened?"

"The battery on the Kawasaki was dead so I replaced it."

"And you thought you had to test it?" Tommy said.

"I felt like a spin up the coast," Victoria said. "I was pulling off by the campsite when I started to feel faint. That's all I remember. I woke up in here."

"Where's the bike? Is it damaged?"

Victoria started to laugh, and a coughing fit ensued. O'Reilly squeezed her hand again.

"It's alright," Victoria managed after a few seconds. "That's my loving brother for you. More worried about a bike that his little sister."

"I didn't mean…"

"The Kawasaki is fine, Tommy," Victoria interrupted. "Apparently it was the first thing I said when I regained consciousness. I asked if the bike was alright. It was put on a trailer and taken to the shop.

That's why we pay insurance."

"There's something wrong with the both of you," O'Reilly said. "Is there time to change my mind about marrying into this family?"

"No chance," Victoria said. "You're part of this family now."

Dr Knight came in and O'Reilly knew what that meant.

"I'll come and see you in the morning," he said to Victoria. "You get some rest."

"Yes dear," she said. "You too. You look tired."

"It's been one of those days."

He kissed her on the forehead and stroked her cheek.

"I'll see you tomorrow," Tommy said. "I might pop to the shop to check on the bike now though."

"I wouldn't expect anything less."

"Are you alright?" Tommy asked O'Reilly as they were walking out.

"Grand," O'Reilly said.

"You don't look well."

"Rough day."

"Vic told me about your wife," Tommy said. "I'm sorry. That must have been rough."

"I didn't handle it well."

"It wasn't your fault."

"No," O'Reilly said. "I could have handled it better. I know you and me haven't always got on, but I'm going to be with Victoria every step of the way. No matter how bad things get. I won't let her down like I let Mary down."

Tommy patted him on the shoulder.
"I know you won't. You're a good man, Liam."
"You're not so bad yourself," O'Reilly said. "It's funny how things turn out, isn't it? Is this the part where we hug like brothers?"
"Don't even think about it."
"I'm glad we're on the same page there."
"I'd better go and see to Vic's bike."
"See you soon," O'Reilly said.

CHAPTER FORTY SIX

O'Reilly was dog tired, but he knew he wouldn't be able to sleep so he got a taxi to the station. He decided that he might as well make himself useful, and he really needed to know what James Green and Sasha Hillman had to say for themselves. He was also curious about the sudden appearance of James's sister, Vanessa. Why had she come back to the island, and what was she doing in the hotel room?

O'Reilly was surprised to see DCI Fish when he walked inside the station. It was clear that the DCI had other things on his mind too.

"Liam," DCI Fish said. "I heard what happened. Is Victoria going to be alright?"

"She'll be fine," O'Reilly said. "She had a dizzy spell while she was out on the bike and she passed out."

"What on earth was she doing on a motorbike in her condition?"

"You should know better than most not to argue with a woman, Tom."

"I won't disagree with that."

"What are you doing here?" O'Reilly asked.

"I had a rather interesting conversation with an old friend. The one I told you about."

He told O'Reilly what he'd learned from Hugh Lincoln.

"It's just as we suspected then," O'Reilly said. "If what your friend said is true and the biggest hurdle is the actual acquisition of the land, we have our motive. At least two of those men were murdered in order to prevent them from throwing a spanner in the works. But if that's the case it leads us to draw only one conclusion. The families of those men are deeply involved."

"That's right," DCI Fish said. "All of them it seems."

"But where does Benjamin Dodds fit into the equation? He didn't own his house – it belongs to his wife. That part of the puzzle doesn't fit."

"No, it doesn't," DCI Fish agreed.

"Although," O'Reilly said. "Mrs Dodds told us she'd sold the house. That's something we need to look into."

"This just gets more and more complicated."

"Have the kids said anything yet?" O'Reilly asked.

"I've only just arrived myself," DCI Fish said. "I came straight here from my friend's house."

"All we need is for one of them to slip up," O'Reilly said. "When more than one person is involved in a murder, the odds of getting one of them to crack are better than with a sole killer."

"Is that the plan of action?"

"I can't think of any other plan of action. We need to keep chipping away at them until one of them breaks. None of the evidence we've gathered points to any of the main suspects – we still haven't finished checking their phones and other electronic devices, but in the meantime, we'll have to do it the hard way."

It didn't take long to ascertain that it wasn't going to be as straightforward as that. All four of the suspects in custody were refusing to say anything. Theresa, Vanessa and James Green were standing firm on this, as was Sasha Hillman. None of them had uttered as much as a *no comment* since they were brought in.

O'Reilly was undeterred. In his experience, when a suspect went that route, it was usually for a damn good reason. It was because they had something to hide, but there were ways to prompt a reaction in someone holding back if you knew which buttons to press. It was for this reason that he decided to formally interview Vanessa Green first. Vanessa had informed them that she wanted a lawyer, and it had to be Stephan Brown. After a two-minute phone call, Vanessa informed O'Reilly that Stephan wouldn't be able to make it until the following morning.

"It looks like you'll be enjoying the hospitality of the Island Police for the night then," he told her.
"You can't do that," she said.
"I can, and I will."
"I haven't done anything."
"I don't believe you," O'Reilly said. "And that's why you'll be spending the night in one of the best holding cells this island has to offer."

Vanessa closed her eyes and put both hands over her face. When she removed them, O'Reilly caught the scent of something sweet. It was a floral scent, and something occurred to him.
"I'll be back," he said and walked off without giving any explanation.

DI Peters informed O'Reilly he would be there in fifteen minutes. From the tone of his voice O'Reilly could tell he wasn't very pleased about being summoned to the station in the middle of the night, but it couldn't be helped. There was something O'Reilly needed to confirm, and he needed it confirmed now.

He used the fifteen minutes to grab a quick cup of tea in his office. He closed the door and savoured the silence. It didn't last long. There was a knock on the door and DC Stone came in.

"What is it, Andy?" O'Reilly said.

"Vanessa Green has a CCTV app on her mobile phone, sir," DC Stone said. "The app is linked to the setup in the secret room at number 2 Rue La Mere."

"Can we tell when she last used it?"

"That's going to take some more time, but we now know it would have been possible for her to access the system remotely."

"Did you find anything else?" O'Reilly asked.

"Nothing. There were a whole load of messages between Sasha and James, but nothing suspicious. Typical teenage stuff."

"Keep looking," O'Reilly said. "None of them are talking, so we need to let the evidence speak for them."

"Is everything alright, sir? I heard about Victoria. Is she going to be alright?"

"She'll be fine, Andy. Thanks for asking. Now, get back to work."

DI Peters arrived twenty minutes later. He wasn't in the best of moods.

"Sorry about this, Jim," O'Reilly said. "But I needed to put my mind at rest."

"It's a bit of a long shot, isn't it?" DI Peters said.

"Sometimes long shots hit the target. Let's hope this is one of those times."

"Where is she?"

"In one of the holding cells," O'Reilly said. "She's not best pleased."

"Let's get this done then, and maybe I can still catch the end of the football game I was watching before I was rudely interrupted."

Vanessa Green was sitting on the hard bed in the holding cell when O'Reilly came back with DI Peters. She looked up at them and smiled.

"No comment."

"Could you get off the bed please," O'Reilly said.

She sighed and did as she was told.

"Are you going to let me out of here?"

"Please step closer to the bars," O'Reilly directed.

"What for?"

"Just do as I say please."

She humoured him. DI Peters stepped closer and sniffed the air close to her face.

Vanessa took a step back.

"What are you, some kind of dirty old man?"

DI Peters ignored her. He turned to O'Reilly and nodded his head.

"As you were," O'Reilly said to Vanessa.

He and DI Peters began walking down the corridor.

"What was that all about?" Vanessa called after them. "You're a pair of dirty old men."

O'Reilly turned around.

"Less of the old," he said.

They continued to walk back towards the main body of the station.

"Are you absolutely sure?" O'Reilly asked DI Peters.

"Positive," he said. "I'd know that scent anywhere. That young woman is wearing Anais Anais."

CHAPTER FORTY SEVEN

O'Reilly stroked Bram's head and Bram let him. The ginger tom wasn't generally a cat who tolerated much affection, but he clearly sensed O'Reilly's mood, and he was sensitive enough to indulge the Irishman. "What a day," O'Reilly said. "Where's your woman?" Right on cue Juliet padded inside the kitchen. She stood next to Bram with her eyes fixed on O'Reilly's. He took the hint and ruffled the fur on her neck.

"We'll be out of here soon, cats. Come September, we'll be moving to the other side of the island. It's as far away as possible from the prat next door and his wimp of a cat."

Bram and Juliet both pricked up their ears and dashed towards the cat flap in the door. O'Reilly assumed they'd heard something outside and gone to investigate.

He looked at the clock on the wall: 11.20. He still wasn't tired, and he knew he'd passed the point where he would be allowed to sleep. There were far too many thoughts bouncing back and forth inside his head, and all of them were vying for O'Reilly's attention. Victoria's accident had thrown him for a six, and it suddenly dawned on him that life was not to be taken for granted. Everything can change in an instant and life can be extinguished as quickly as it arrived. It was a depressing thought.

A screech outside interrupted his thought process and he let it. The cats were fighting again. He envied them. Theirs was a simple life – eat, sleep, repeat. Perhaps with the occasional altercation thrown in for good measure. O'Reilly had never believed in reincarnation, but he decided that if there was such a thing, when he came back in his next life, he would like to be born a cat. Everything would be so much easier.

His phone pinged to tell him he'd received a message. He swiped the screen and saw it was

Assumpta. He was surprised she was still awake, but then he remembered it was Saturday. She didn't have to work tomorrow. He opened the message and read it. Assumpta was asking if Victoria was OK. DC Stone must have told her what happened.

O'Reilly didn't feel like explaining via a string of messages. He brought up her number and pressed *call*.

She picked up straight away.

"Andy told me about the accident," she said. "Is Victoria alright?"

"She's fine," O'Reilly told her. "She had a funny turn on the bike, but she wasn't going very fast, and her injuries weren't serious. She lost consciousness, but she's on the mend now."

"What made her pass out?"

"The docs are doing some tests," O'Reilly said. "But they think it was probably a side-effect of the radiation treatment. They'll be keeping her in for a while."

"How are *you* doing?" Assumpta said.

"Knackered," O'Reilly said. "And unable to sleep. This investigation has been draining."

"Have you made any progress?"

"It's confusing. We know what it's all about, but

everything has been meticulously planned, and we have nothing concrete to put anyone in the picture for the murders. I've never come across anything like it before."

"Andy and me are throwing a party next weekend," Assumpta changed the subject. "A sort of housewarming thing."

"Grand," O'Reilly said. "Am I invited?"

"Of course you're invited, Dad. It'll be nothing fancy. Just a few friends and work colleagues."

"I'll be moving to Vazon after the wedding."

"Where did that come from?"

"It seemed like the logical thing to do. Victoria loves her house, and I've got no ties to my place. Plus, the prat who lives next door is really starting to get on my nerves. He never stops moaning about his pathetic little cat."

"That's great news."

Something occurred to O'Reilly. He didn't know why it came to him right then, but he recalled the conversation with Fred Viking earlier and he remembered he'd made some kind of verbal agreement with the unscrupulous editor. He was in a bit of a predicament. The rational side of his brain was telling him not to honour the agreement. It would be tantamount to selling his soul to the devil, but his conscience was telling him otherwise. A deal is a deal, and a man does not go back on his word. But there was a way to appease both his conscience and the voice of reason inside his head in one fell swoop.

"Summi," he said. "I've got some information for you that you might find interesting."

"Are you sure you want to do this, Dad?" she said.

"I am. But you did not get this from me."

"I'm not a wet-behind-the-ears trainee journalist."

"Fair enough. We've had word that there are plans to build a hotel in Vazon. And this is not just any old hotel – this is a hotel the likes of which the island has never seen before. Rumour has it the investors in the project already have a buyer lined up. A French billionaire is rumoured to be willing to part with half a billion for it."

"Why are you telling me this?" Assumpta asked.

"Hear me out. The hotel I'm talking about is to be built on a site currently occupied by three houses. Three exclusive properties on a piece of prime real estate. The houses I'm referring to are numbers 2, 4, and 6 Rue La Mere."

"This is huge, Dad."

"It's even bigger than that," O'Reilly said. "Three men

have been murdered and the conspiracy to kill them involves a whole team of plotters. This is the most carefully orchestrated string of murders any of us have ever come across, and when the truth gets out it's going to send shockwaves across the island for years."

The line was silent for a while.

"Are you still there?" O'Reilly asked.

"I'm still here. I'm trying to get my head round this. Are you telling me those men were killed so whoever is planning on building the hotel can get hold of their land?"

"That's exactly what I'm telling you, Summi. And there's more. The families of those men are all involved. We know of at least four of them who are a big part of this. Theresa, Vanessa and James Green are in custody as we speak, as is Sasha Hillman. We can't pin anything on any of them yet because they've done a grand job of covering their tracks, but I'm confident we'll get one of them to crack. That's all we need. When one of them cracks the others will follow."

"Why are you telling me this, Dad?" Assumpta said.

"I have my reasons," O'Reilly replied. "But you need to act on this quickly. This isn't going to stay a secret for long. You need to work on something as soon as we get off the phone."

"Does anyone else know about this?"

"It's only a matter of time," O'Reilly said.

"This is massive. I'll work through the night if I have to. Fiona won't mind being woken up with this kind of news. I'll make sure this goes out in tomorrow's Sunday edition."

"And, Summi…"

"Don't worry," she interrupted. "Whatever I put out will not be traced back to you in any way."

"I sincerely hope not," O'Reilly said. "Because I dread to think what will happen if it does."

"This is the story of the decade, Dad."

"I'd say it's the story of the century. This is murder for money on a scale that's never been seen before on the island. There is evil at play here that defies belief."

"Thank you," Assumpta said. "I don't know why you're telling me all this but thank you."

"I'll let you get started," O'Reilly said. "I'll see you when I see you."

He ended the call and rubbed his eyes. Weariness was creeping up on him now, and he knew he needed to get some sleep. He looked at the phone on the table and sighed. Then he picked it up and dialled Fred

Viking's number. The editor of the Island Herald picked up after a few seconds – O'Reilly explained the nature of the call and gave him an abridged version of what he'd just told his daughter.

CHAPTER FORTY EIGHT

The last day of June was a day O'Reilly would remember for the rest of his life. The day that marked the halfway point in the year 2019 would be a day that would be imprinted on his brain until he drew his final breath.

It was gone midnight before he finally went to bed, but he still woke early feeling remarkably refreshed. He wasn't sure if this was because his conscience was clear, or if there was another reason for the sudden heightened alertness. He got out of bed, dressed and prepared to face whatever the day threw his way.

He got to the station just before eight and he was surprised to find that he was the last one to arrive. The whole team had got there before him. After a quick cup of tea and a brief check of his emails O'Reilly headed straight to the briefing room. They had a lot to discuss before they could proceed with the interviews of the four suspects who'd spent the night at the station.

The tired eyes of the people sitting around the table told O'Reilly that he wasn't the only one who'd had a late night. DC Stone looked like he was about to fall asleep at any moment. His rat-like eyes were mere dots, and his hair was unwashed. DC Owen also looked exhausted. Her eyes were bloodshot and there were heavy bags below them. DS Skinner didn't look like he was bearing up much better. DCI Fish wasn't there.

"Morning," O'Reilly said and sat down. "I trust you all got some rest."

"Not really, sir." It was DC Stone. "I called it a night at around three when I couldn't keep my eyes open anymore."

"I managed to stay awake until four," DC Owen added.

"Did you spend the night here?" O'Reilly asked.

"It seemed pointless going home," DC Owen said. "I grabbed a few hours' sleep on a chair."

"We have four suspects to grill this morning," O'Reilly said. "It's highly likely they're going to keep quiet, and that's why we need something to throw at them in case they do. Does anyone have anything that might fit the bill?"

"Vanessa Green's phone gave us something, sir," DC Stone said. "She was using a Thai network until last Wednesday. There was nothing on her phone until late Wednesday night, and then the network was changed to a UK one."

"She flew out on Wednesday then," O'Reilly deduced. "Can we tell from her phone if she was on the island on the morning her father was murdered?"

"Unfortunately not, sir," DC Stone said. "All we know is she was using a UK mobile phone network."

"Damn it," O'Reilly said. "She could argue that she was actually in the UK, and we have no way to disprove it. Anything else?"

None of them got the chance to say anything further. DCI Fish marched in and the expression on his face told its own story. He looked absolutely furious. He was holding a newspaper in his hand.

He flung it down on the table. "What the hell is this?"

It was the Sunday edition of the Guernsey Gazette. The headline on the front grabbed the attention immediately.

Evil on the Island.

Below the headline was a photograph of a hotel. It was a grand looking hotel, and O'Reilly assumed that Assumpta had used a bit of artistic license there. The hotel that was at the heart of all this wasn't even built yet.

"Where the hell did they get this information?" DCI Fish addressed the question to nobody in particular.

"What's in the article?" DC Stone asked.

"Everything we've discussed in the past few days," DCI Fish replied. "This isn't a simple case of having a source on the inside – everything we know is on the front page of the local newspaper. Where did they get this from?"

O'Reilly decided to take a chance. He knew he was taking a huge risk in doing so, but he decided it was worth it.

He raised his hand. "Guilty as charged." Everyone turned to look at him. DCI Fish opened his mouth to speak but no words came out. His mouth remained open, and for a moment he really did resemble his name. He put O'Reilly in mind of a fish in a tank. A guppy perhaps.

"What the devil were you thinking, Liam?" DCI Fish found his voice at last.

"Desperate times call for desperate measures, Tom," O'Reilly said.

"Would you care to explain what you mean by that?"

O'Reilly tapped the newspaper. "This has brought it out into the open. The closely kept secret of the hotel project is no longer a secret. By lunchtime today every man, woman and child on this island is going to know about this, and that's going to change the game in our favour."

"How do you figure that out?" DCI Fish said. "This is going to cause major problems for us. This is a headache we can do without. You'll be lucky to come out of this with your job intact, Liam. I can't protect you from the backlash that's going to come out of this."

"I don't need your protection," O'Reilly said. "This is going to cause some cracks in the armour of everyone involved in the despicable plot. One of them is going to break and that's all we need. The truth is out there, and they won't have been expecting it. This is going to work in our favour."

"I hope to God you're right," DCI Fish said.

He looked around the room at the team gathered there.

He sighed deeply. "We need to discuss damage control."

"I'm man enough to take it on the chin, Tom," O'Reilly said.

"I don't doubt that, but that's precisely what you're not going to do. The only people who know where the Gazette got their info from are right here in this room, and that's how it's going to stay."

"I can't ask any of you to lie for me," O'Reilly said.

"We can't afford to lose you, Liam," DCI Fish said.

"I have no idea where the Gazette got the info from," DC Stone said and rubbed his eyes.

"Me neither," DS Skinner added.

"It was probably one of the uniforms," DC Owen suggested. "It usually is."

O'Reilly smiled. He studied the tired faces of his colleagues and a warm feeling started to build inside him. It spread upwards from his stomach, and he could feel his neck flush.

"Thank you."

"Let's move on," DCI Fish said.

"Before we do," O'Reilly said. "There's something else I suppose I ought to tell you. The Gazette isn't the only one privy to this information – I gave Fred Viking a bit of a head's-up too."

CHAPTER FORTY NINE

"Interview with Vanessa Green commenced, 9:15," O'Reilly began. "The date is June 30th. Present Miss Green, DI O'Reilly, DC Owen and Miss Green's legal representative Stephan Brown. Miss Green, I trust you slept well."

"We will be taking this further," Stephan said. "Your treatment of my client is disgusting. You had no grounds to hold her like a caged dog, and there will be serious repercussions coming your way from that."

"Have you finished?" O'Reilly said. "Your client is suspected of committing a serious crime. She has thus far refused to prove otherwise, so I am well within my rights to detain her until I'm satisfied she played no part in that crime. And you know full well I am."

"Can we just get on with it?" Vanessa said. "I want to get out of here."

"Miss Green," O'Reilly said.

"Could you please call me Vanessa. Miss Green makes me sound like a schoolteacher."

"Vanessa," O'Reilly humoured her. "You flew out to Thailand last week, is that correct?"

"What has my trip to Thailand got to do with anything?"

"Just answer the question," DC Owen said.

"I flew out a week ago."

"What happened over there?" O'Reilly said. "What made you come back so soon?"

"I was bored."

"Bored," O'Reilly repeated. "I think you're lying."

"Whatever."

"I think you went to Thailand to give you an alibi for the time your father was killed. The time he was brutally murdered. He sustained more than a dozen stab wounds to his neck, face and stomach."

"That's enough," Stephan said. "Miss Brown does not need to know the gory details."

"She already knows the details," O'Reilly said. "I can guarantee you she already knows. Let's go back to Thailand. You flew out last Sunday and returned on Wednesday, is that correct? Be careful here. It'll be easy to check."

"So what? I got a flight back on Wednesday."

"You flew into Heathrow," DC Owen said. "Is that right?"

"What about it?" Vanessa said.

"And you came back to the island straight afterwards," O'Reilly said. "Is that also correct."

"No."

"You didn't come back to Guernsey?" O'Reilly said.

"Obviously I did come back to the island," Vanessa said. "I'm here now, aren't I? But I only got back on Friday."

"The day after Mr Green was killed," Stephan Brown pointed out.

"OK," O'Reilly said. "You claim to have got back on Friday. There's something I'm finding hard to fathom. Why did you not make contact with your family? Surely you must have heard about what happened to your father by then. Why not get in touch with you mother and brother?"

"Who says I didn't?" Vanessa said.

"Are you claiming to have contacted them?" DC Owen said.

"Of course. What kind of cold-hearted person do you think I am?"

"That has yet to be decided," O'Reilly said.

"Ask them," Vanessa said. "Ask Mum and James. They'll confirm it."

O'Reilly didn't doubt that. He wasn't going to get any further with this topic of conversation.

"When you returned to the island," he said. "You carried on using your phone with a UK network. Why is that?"

"I didn't get round to changing it back," Vanessa said.

"I find that hard to believe. You've lived on the island your whole life. Surely your default network would be a Guernsey one."

"I didn't know how long I'd be away."

"What is the relevance of this?" Stephan asked.

"It's probably not important."

"Then may I ask you to keep your line of questioning relevant to the matter at hand?"

"Vanessa," O'Reilly said. "Are you aware that there are plans to build an upmarket hotel on the site where you currently reside?"

"What on earth has that got to do with this investigation?" Stephan said.

"Answer the question, Vanessa," DC Owen said.

"Your reaction was quite obvious," O'Reilly said. "You might think you've covered your tracks. You might believe you've considered every eventual outcome, but it's virtually impossible to maintain a poker face twenty-four-seven. You're human and you're still young. You weren't expecting the question, and you reacted instinctively."

"I have no idea what you're talking about," Vanessa said.

"You're lying. You're good, but you're not that good. The hotel has been approved. The project has been given the green light, but for work to begin the land needs to be acquired."

"No comment."

"Seeing as the cat's got your tongue," O'Reilly said. "I'll do the talking, shall I? This is what I think happened. I think you came back from Thailand and headed straight back to the island. You didn't tell anybody apart from your family you were back, and you put stage one of your plan into action. You somehow lured your father to the house on Rue La Mere, and you killed him. James discovered the body and set the ball rolling."

"I've never heard anything so ludicrous in my life," Stephan Brown said.

"You cleaned yourself up," O'Reilly carried on. "And you drove your mother's Audi to her tennis club, making sure to leave the knife in the glove compartment."

"Prove it," Vanessa said.

"There are CCTV cameras overlooking the car park at the tennis club," DC Owen said. "They caught you leaving the car."

"You're doing it again, Vanessa," O'Reilly said. "You might not think so, but you reacted to what my colleague just told you. It was a subtle change on your face, but I've had years of practice in stuff like that."

"Why hasn't the CCTV footage come up before?" Stephan asked.

"Where's the fun in that?" O'Reilly said. "Moving on. Later that day you came back to Rue La Mere. You knew John Hillman was planning on playing golf and you were aware that he would be home alone. I believe Sasha Hillman gave you this information. Miss Hillman is being interviewed as we speak, and I'm positive she'll confirm it. You killed Mr Hillman and left him in the hallway for Sasha to find later."

"I presume you have something that proves this?" Stephan said.

"Not yet, but the odds are in our favour. One of you is going to crack – it's just a question of who cracks first."

"Is this farce going to take much longer?" Stephan asked. "Nothing you've put forward so far can be linked to my client. You cannot prove anything."

"Please bear with me," O'Reilly said. "Vanessa, you knew that Benjamin Dodds played bowls on a Friday. Has done for years. You followed him there and waited for the opportunity to kill him. You wore gloves when you bashed his head in with the bowls ball, and you'd already transferred your mother's fingerprints onto it. That part was good by the way. I don't mind admitting, that was rather ingenious."

"This is laughable," Vanessa said.

"I'm afraid my sense of humour took a bit of a dip when I realised this was all about money. It's a disgusting amount of money – I'll give you that, but murder for money has always been a particular bane of mine. It tends to leave a bad taste in my mouth. Is there anything you'd like to say, Vanessa?"

She smiled and rolled her eyes.

"No comment."

CHAPTER FIFTY

O'Reilly was having a cup of tea in his office when DCI Fish came in. It was just after one and the morning hadn't been as productive as O'Reilly would have hoped. He knew all four of the people they'd spoken to were involved in the three murders, but nothing that had come out of the interviews gave them anything to confirm it beyond a shadow of a doubt. DCI Fish wasn't about to make things any better. He was the bearer of bad news.

"We have to release them. We cannot justify holding them any longer."

"We have reasonable grounds," O'Reilly argued. "I just need some more time. Let me have another crack at

Vanessa. She was close to losing it, and I know I can break her."

"Listen to yourself, Liam. You're talking like a desperate man."

"Three men are dead, and the people responsible are in this station right now. We cannot let them go."

"I'm on the same page as you, but unless we have more proof, we don't have a choice. All we have is a bowling ball with the fingerprints of a woman who was in police custody the time the murder was carried out. We've got nothing."

O'Reilly knew DCI Fish was right, but he wasn't happy about it.

"We'll keep digging," DCI Fish said. "Those four aren't going anywhere. They'll be on the island if we need them. We'll find something that implicates them in this, but for now we have to let them go."

His phone started to ring in his pocket. He took it out and looked at the screen.

"I have to take this," he said to O'Reilly. "It's Hugh Lincoln. The friend I told you about."

He answered the phone and left O'Reilly alone with his thoughts.

Those thoughts were more jumbled than ever, and he was prevented from putting them into some semblance of order when his phone started to ring. The screen told him it was a call he'd been expecting.

"You screwed me over, O'Reilly."

"It's good to hear from you too, Fred," O'Reilly said.

"You promised me that what you told me was exclusively mine."

"I promised you nothing of the kind."

"You said it was the scoop of the century. That implies that it was my scoop and my scoop alone. You're a conniving Irish bastard."

"I've been called worse," O'Reilly said. "Will there be anything else?"

"This isn't over, O'Reilly. This isn't over by a long shot. Your superiors are going to hear about this."

"I very much doubt that."

"Watch me. You're going to regret the day you thought you could double-cross Fred Viking. I am an enemy you definitely do not want to have on this island."

"That's better," O'Reilly said. "Things are back to normal again. It didn't feel right to be exchanging pleasantries with you. It gave me an uncomfortable feeling in my stomach. Good luck, Viking."

He hung up and stretched his arms. The argument with Fred *the Ed* felt good. It felt like things were back on track between him and the editor. It wasn't right to be on friendly terms with a man like Fred Viking.

DCI Fish came back in and this time it was quite clear he wasn't bringing bad news with him. He was grinning like a lunatic, and he was holding a piece of paper in his hand.

"We've got a lead," he said. "A real humdinger of a lead."

"What have you got there?" O'Reilly pointed to the paper.

"A printout of an email Hugh sent over. And it makes for disturbing reading."

He sat down opposite O'Reilly at his desk.

"Hugh did some digging and, after a bit of persuasion he managed to get some answers about the consortium involved in the development of the hotel."

"Do we have any names?" O'Reilly asked.

"The company is registered in the Cayman Islands," DCI Fish said.

"Untraceable then."

"Nothing is untraceable, Liam. It just means that if or when this gets to court, things become rather complicated, but this is a real breakthrough. The consortium of investors set the ball rolling over a year ago. The architectural plans for the hotel were already complete, and potential buyers were propositioned."

"It's supposed to be some rich French bloke."

"That's neither here nor there," DCI Fish said. "The French billionaire hasn't committed a crime. The deal is legit, but the development phase is far from it. The land on Rue La Mere had to be acquired, and we all know how that was achieved."

O'Reilly certainly did.

"The consortium is structured the same as any company would be," DCI Fish continued. "There's a board with a director at the helm. In this instance it appears that's simply for appearances sake. All the board members are actually on an equal standing, and all of them have an equal share in the so-called company."

"Who's on the board?" O'Reilly asked. "Who stands to gain from this hotel being built?"

"I don't know all the details," DCI Fish said. "The consortium are not obliged to make that knowledge public. It's not a listed company."

"How is that going to help us? How can it be considered a breakthrough?"

"Because Hugh knows people who know things, Liam."

"And?"

"The legal team representing the consortium are known to us," DCI Fish said. "They're here on the island."

"Brown and Henshaw?" O'Reilly guessed.

"The very same," DCI Fish confirmed. "And the person at the helm of the board of directors is also known to us. It's someone we haven't even considered yet."

"I'm afraid I can't guess that one," O'Reilly admitted.

"Jane Dodds," DCI Fish said. "The person at the head of the consortium responsible for the deaths of three men is an old woman."

* * *

"I don't think she's going to give us any grief," O'Reilly said.

He and DC Owen were parked once again on Rue La Mere. Backup was in place further up the street, but O'Reilly didn't think it was really necessary. Jane Dodds was hardly a threat to any of them. She was sixty years old, and she would be easy to overpower.

"I never expected this in a million years," DC Owen said. "We didn't even think about Jane Dodds."

"We've been well and truly flummoxed, Katie," O'Reilly admitted. "Flummoxed by a harmless old lady. Let's go and have a chat with her."

Jane Dodds opened the door so quickly O'Reilly suspected she was expecting them.

He was right.

"I was wondering when you'd show up."

She smiled at O'Reilly. He didn't reciprocate.

"Mrs Dodds," he said. "You're going to have to come with us."

"I don't think so," she said.

"I'm afraid it isn't up for debate. You need to come with us."

"That's not how it's supposed to be."

"That's how it's going to be," O'Reilly insisted. "Don't make this any harder than it already is."

"No," Jane said. "No, no, no. Come in. We'll talk inside. The kettles just boiled. I'll make us all a nice cup of tea. Or something stronger if you like."

"Mrs Dodds," O'Reilly said. "The whole street is swarming with Island Police. You're coming with us."

He wasn't expecting what happened next. Jane slipped her hand behind her and pulled out a gun. O'Reilly recognised it as a Smith and Wesson .38 Special.

"Don't do this," he said.

Jane looked at the gun and shook her head.

"This isn't for you, dear. Come in, and I'll tell you everything you want to know."

CHAPTER FIFTY ONE

One year earlier

"Help yourself to some nibbles."

Jane Dodds had laid out quite a spread. There were sandwiches of all kinds - sausage rolls, cheese sticks, mini pies, and a whole host of other delicious snacks. Nobody touched the food.

"The plans for the most extravagant hotel this island has ever seen have been approved. Pascal DeJour has confirmed his interest with an offer to purchase and the ball has been well and truly set in motion. Now we need to put all our efforts into the land. You all know what your individual roles are. Are there any questions?"

"Just one." It was Theresa Green. "What happens if we get caught?"

"We will not get caught," Jane said. "If everything is done as discussed we will not get caught."

"Could you talk us through it again?" James Green said.

Sasha Hillman gave him a playful slap on the shoulder. "We've only spoken about it, like a million times."

"James is right," his sister, Vanessa said. "I think we should go over it once more."

"Stephan," Jane said. "Would you be so kind?"

"My pleasure," the experienced lawyer obliged. "The most important aspect of the plan is to be ready when the time comes. Vanessa, you need to be prepared to get off the island at the drop of a hat. Make sure your passport is up to date, and make sure you're not travelling alone. You need to ensure that it looks like you were miles away when the curtains go up, and the action begins."

"I'm not sure I'll be able to lie to the police," James said.

"That's why your role in this is a minor one," Stephan told him. "All you have to do is stumble across the body of your father. I don't think that's an awful lot to ask. Practice deceit in the mirror if you have to. This will only work if everyone sticks to their part of the plan. One mistake and it's game over. Arnold will be dispatched first. James will make the gruesome discovery and it's all systems go. Theresa, you will be elsewhere when the murder is carried out, but it's important you cannot provide a watertight alibi. There must be room for doubt if the murder weapon in your car is to be believed."

James Green helped himself to a pie. He finished it off in two bites.

"John Hillman will be taken out next," Stephan continued. "It's vitally important that Theresa is missing in action when his murder is carried out. By then, the Island Police will be out looking for her, but it is equally important that they don't locate her. Theresa, you will go to them when the time's right. By then confusion will have set in. The Island Police are not ace detectives but they're not stupid either. We just need to spread the confusion and have them running after false leads until this is all over."

"Why do I have to do the killing?" Vanessa asked.
"We've been over this," Stephan said. "You're the most suitable. You're the one who can focus on the prey and go in for the kill without emotion getting in the way. That is a rare talent."
"What?" James said. "Being a psychopath is considered a talent?"
"That's enough," Stephan said. "Only when Theresa is in custody is Benjamin Dodds to be added to the list of victims. I do not need to stress the importance of that."

"Is the buyer definitely serious?" Theresa asked.
"Mr DeJour is one hundred percent on board," Stephan confirmed. "We have the offer to purchase at the offices of Brown and Henshaw. When this is over

all of you inside this room will be extremely wealthy. You will all receive somewhere close to one-hundred-million pounds. But you will have to work hard to earn that money."

He looked at his watch. "I must be going. I have a meeting with a client in an hour. You all know what's expected of you."

CHAPTER FIFTY TWO

"And that's how it was planned?" O'Reilly said. "At a soiree in your living room. You orchestrated a plan that involved killing three men around a table of snacks?"

"It all boils down to common etiquette," Jane said. The .38 Special was on the table in front of her. O'Reilly debated whether to make a grab for it, but he decided it was too risky. Jane Dodds was getting on in years, but she was still a sharp cookie.

"There are a few aspects of this I find it hard to understand," O'Reilly said.

"You have my full attention," Jane said.

She cast a glance at the gun, and O'Reilly sensed she wouldn't hesitate to use it if necessarily.

"Why kill Benjamin?" he said. "He was declared bankrupt. He had nothing. Why did you kill your husband?"

"I didn't kill him."

"You were part of the conspiracy, Jane. You may as well have bashed his head in yourself. Why did Benjamin have to die?"

"He was suffering from doubts. That wouldn't do. That hotel has been my dream for years, and I couldn't let anything get in the way of it."

"You plotted to murder your husband for the sake of a stupid hotel?" DC Owen said.

"You watch your mouth, young lady. It is not a stupid hotel. That hotel would have been spectacular. And part of the deal was I would be given a permanent room there. Spectacular."

O'Reilly was finding it hard to digest all of this. Three men had lost their lives because of one woman's desire to see a hotel built.

"Mrs Dodds," he said. "You are possibly the most despicable human being I have ever met. Evil doesn't even come close."

"The likes of you wouldn't understand," Jane said.

"The likes of me have a thing called a conscience. And while we're on the topic, how did you manage to persuade everybody else to play along? Murder for money is one thing, but I've never seen a conspiracy to kill involving so many parties. How was that even possible? This was evil on a grand scale."

"Mental manipulation is my forte," Jane said. "I have a natural gift for it. You just have to understand which buttons to press. Vanessa killed her father. You may find that difficult to comprehend, but it was relatively easy to get her to do that. The man was a dog. He treated the family like dirt and when he got together with the tart Vanessa was especially pliable."

"And James?" DC Owen said. "Was he also pliable?"

Jane started to laugh. It was rather disturbing under the circumstances.

"Ah, James," she said. "That boy is like any teenage boy. Driven by a pair of tits and a pretty face."

O'Reilly was shocked by her words.

"It's the truth," Jane said. "James is smitten with Sasha, and Sasha, in turn happens to despise her father. Like I said, you push the right buttons, and you can dictate the action every time. I'm sure I don't have to explain how I got Theresa on board."

"When did you come up with this evil plan?" O'Reilly asked.

"A little over a year ago," Jane said. "It was serendipity if you like. I received an email from Stephan at Brown and Henshaw. He informed me of a potential money spinner. Little did I know then that it would be so lucrative."

"But it wasn't, was it?" DC Owen said. "Three men are dead, and your hotel is never going to be built. Was it worth it? Was it worth losing your husband over?"

"Don't be so melodramatic. Benjamin was a useless man. Always has been. His father warned me about him, but I didn't listen."

"I'm starting to feel slightly ill," O'Reilly said.

"I'm not going to jail," Jane said. "I won't go to jail."

"I'm afraid you don't have a choice," O'Reilly said. "You and your co-conspirators will spend most of the rest of your lives behind bars. Was it worth it?"

"I will not rot away in a prison cell. I have the children to consider. Think of the shame."

"You didn't consider your children when you murdered their father," DC Owen said.

"They're better off without him. You can leave me in peace now."

"You know that's not going to happen," O'Reilly said. "I think we're done here. Come on, Jane – there's nowhere left to run."

"I'm not sorry you know."

Jane Dodds reached for the Smith and Wesson .38 Special. She looked O'Reilly in the eye, raised the gun and fired a bullet through her left temple.

CHAPTER FIFTY THREE

"A conspiracy of evil."

DCI Fish was the first to speak after listening to the confession of Jane Dodds. DC Owen had had the presence of mind to turn on the voice recorder on her phone when she realised the woman behind the conspiracy had no intention of telling her story in a police interview room.

That voice recording was instrumental. Vanessa Green had been charged with three counts of murder. Theresa and James were facing conspiracy charges for the same crimes, as were Sasha Hillman and Stephan Brown. All of them were facing lengthy prison terms. The reality of what happened hadn't yet hit home on the island, but it was only a matter of time before the shockwaves spread.

"The bitch took the easy way out." It was DC Stone.

"That's enough, Andy," O'Reilly warned.

"It's true. She should have rotted in jail for what she did. Shooting herself was a cop-out."

"It is what it is," O'Reilly said.

"I don't need to remind you about the workload this is going to give us in the coming weeks," DCI Fish said. "There is a mountain of paperwork to deal with now."

"Great," DC Stone said.

"That can wait," O'Reilly decided. "Tomorrow is another day."

"We need to make a start on it now, Liam," DCI Fish argued.

O'Reilly stood up. "I disagree, Tom. It's Sunday, and we're all knackered. As the officer in charge of the investigation I'm putting my foot down. You're all officially on enforced leave until nine, tomorrow morning. If anyone has a problem with that, tough luck. I'll see you in the morning."

He left the briefing room and headed outside into the sunshine. He'd no sooner stepped outside when his phone started to ring. He answered it without checking to see who it was. That was a big mistake.
"Your cats have gone too far this time, Mr O'Reilly."
"Good," O'Reilly found himself saying.
"My poor Timothy won't stop shaking. This is not on. It's your last warning. If those thugs of yours persist in the persecution I shall have no choice but to involve the authorities."
"Feck this," O'Reilly said and ended the call.

DC Stone came outside and walked over to O'Reilly.
"That's that then. It's all over."
"You did some good work there, Andy," O'Reilly told him. "The whole team deserve a great big pat on the back. Can I trouble you for a lift?"
"No trouble, sir. Do you want me to drop you off at home?"

"Hospital," O'Reilly said. "I've made a decision and I need a second opinion."

DC Stone gave O'Reilly a puzzled look, but he didn't press further.

* * *

"What brought this on?"

Victoria Radcliffe looked much better today. She'd enjoyed a good nights' sleep, and she was looking forward to going home. The tests the doctors had done confirmed there wasn't anything to worry about. The dizzy spell was a common side-effect of the radiation treatment, and the medical specialists had advised Victoria not to ride her motorbike until the course of radiation was finished. She'd reluctantly agreed.

"Well?" she said to O'Reilly. "What's brought this on?"

"An unrelated series of events," he said. "A glimpse at the dark side of human nature, the realisation that life is not to be taken for granted, and a pedantic neighbour with a lily-livered cat."

Victoria started to laugh. "I'm not sure we'll be able to arrange things at such short notice."

"A lot can be achieved in a week," O'Reilly said. "The Bay Hotel in Albecq is available next Saturday. I've provisionally booked the reception hall."

"You never cease to surprise me, Liam O'Reilly."

"They'll provide the catering, the entertainment, everything. All you need to do is get hold of a dress and show up on time."

"Are you sure this is the right thing to do?" Victoria asked.

"I've never been so sure of anything in my life. Why wait three months? I want to be your husband now. I want to move in with you now."

"What about your landlord? Don't you have to give some sort of notice?"

"Don't worry about the landlord. I've got a feeling he'll be glad to be rid of me. What do you say?"

"What do I say?" Victoria repeated. "What the hell – let's do this."

CHAPTER FIFTY FOUR

"Your boss is a shit dancer."

Tommy Radcliffe was standing with DC Owen. They'd got chatting and they'd hit it off from the very start. The wedding reception was underway, and O'Reilly was trying his best not to embarrass himself on the dancefloor. It was the first dance with his new wife.

"O'Reilly's talents lie elsewhere," DC Owen said.

"Thank God for that," Tommy said. "Because he can't dance to save his life."

The song ended and O'Reilly was glad. He'd never been a big fan of dancing, and he was relieved the first dance was over. He kissed Victoria on the cheek and told her he was going to speak to DC Owen.

"You two seem to be getting on well," he said.

"Tommy was just complementing you on your dance moves," DC Owen said.

"I bet he was. Are you sorted for drinks?"

"Tommy has been keeping me well watered."

Victoria's brother held out his hand. "Welcome to the family."

O'Reilly shook the hand. "I'm proud to be a part of it. You're stuck with me now."

"I can think of worse brothers in law. Have you given any more thought about getting back on a bike?"

"I need to buy one first."

"Then it's your lucky day. We had a clean Rebel come in during the week. I can give it to you for a good price."

"I'll give it some serious consideration. I'd better get back to my wife."

"That's going to take a bit of getting used to."

Victoria was otherwise engaged when O'Reilly went to find her. She was dancing with a man O'Reilly didn't recognise. He got himself a beer from the bar and watched her dance. She really was very good, and he debated whether to improve his game in that department. He decided it would be a fruitless endeavour. He'd always had two left feet – that was just the way it was.

The song ended and Victoria and the mystery man walked over to O'Reilly.

"Liam," she said. "This is Daniel, my cousin. Daniel, meet my husband."

"Good to meet you, Liam," Daniel said. "Victoria has told me all about you."

"All good stuff, I hope."

"Nothing but."

"Can I leave you two gentlemen for a minute?" Victoria said. "I need to use the Ladies."

"Don't be long," O'Reilly said.

"Victoria told me you work for the Island Police," Daniel said.

"That's right," O'Reilly said.

"Detective Inspector."

"Also correct."

"That's quite impressive," Daniel said. "You must earn a few bob then?"

O'Reilly wasn't expecting this. "Not as much as you'd think. What do you do?"

"Investment banking. Actually I might have a proposition for you if you're looking to invest."

"I'm not," O'Reilly said, rather bluntly.

"You'd be a fool to pass this one up. This is still hush hush, but you look like a man who can keep his mouth shut. There's a construction project in the pipeline up in Beaucette. Right by the marina there. They're planning on building a luxury hotel."

"I'm not interested," O'Reilly said.

"Hear me out. This isn't just any old hotel. You put your money into this, and you'll be a very happy man at the end."

"I'm not interested," O'Reilly said once more.

"It's your funeral," Daniel said.

"And I'll leave this mortal coil with a clear conscience," O'Reilly said. "Good luck, Daniel."

THE END

Printed in Great Britain
by Amazon